Neutral Space

Rebecca Tran

Published by R Tran Books, 2018.

NEUTRAL SPACE

First edition. January 11, 2018.

Copyright © 2018 Rebecca Tran.

ISBN: 979-8230201175

Written by Rebecca Tran.

Chapter 1

My name is Jackson Eli Peterson, and this is my true story. Not the story the human and the Kelsairan governments want you to believe. I was born and raised on Sirus Seven, otherwise known as Greed to the humans. Each of the seven inhabitable planets of the Sirus system was renamed for the seven deadly sins of the Bible. They were after all the starting point of the war between the Kelsairans and the humans. A war, I might add, that has become a way of life for both races over the past two hundred years.

The humans began their colonization effort in the year 2655. It began with the Hyperion system closer to Earth and had mild success. It was then that the Kelsairans took an interest in humans. They had done the same thing and wanted to share their technology; of course, they tried to make a nice profit in the process. So, the trading began, and both races prospered. Humans spread to other systems and had five colonized planets in 50 years. Then, civil unrest led to civil war on Kelsair. Trade was suspended, and each race went on with their own business.

When the new Kelsairan government rose out of the ashes of the old, it looked to the humans once again to start trade. But the humans no longer needed the Kelsairans. A group of planets was promised to the humans to entice them back into trade agreements. The Sirus system was abandoned during their civil war, and seven inhabitable planets so close to one another proved too appetizing to be overlooked. The deal was signed. The Sirus system became a human territory.

That is how it remained for nearly a century. Then the Kelsairans sent an embassy to Earth, and all hell broke loose. They demanded the return of the Sirus system stating that the human tenancy was at an end. The president, of course, refused. The trade agreements said nothing about the humans being tenants; not to mention it would have displaced three billion people. And so the war began, and it hasn't stopped since.

It's May 18, 3006 now and I find myself at the end of a strange and undistinguished career in the army. I am not old enough to retire nor am I wounded. I have not finished my contract, yet my career is over all the same. There are many reasons I left the army. But, I'm afraid none of them would make sense unless you read my story as I lived it; starting from the point when I realized something was wrong with everything I knew.

Two years ago my unit was on a reconnaissance mission on the third moon around Cemes; a planet on the border of Kelsairan and Human territories. There was supposed to be a munitions storage, our job was to find the warehouse and get out. We were ambushed and took heavy fire. My men managed to escape. I woke up on a Kelsairan transport with a pounding headache.

The man next to me smelled from weeks of confinement, but at least he was human. "Friend, where are we going?" I asked.

"Don't know, I don't speak their trash."

"Kras," the man across the row offered. Kras damn it. That was the last place we wanted to go. "It's good news Kelsairan jails are bound to be better than any they would put just humans."

The man was trying to cheer me up I knew. Kras wasn't any Kelsairan prison it was for their hardened prisoners, and we would not be given separate cells. These men may have a chance of living they didn't look to be military. If the Kelsairans realized I was, they would attack me on the spot just out of spite. I managed a smile for the man hoping I would make it to my first meal.

"What branch are you, boy?" another man asked.

"Army,"

"The guards have been by three times to check on you already."

"Surprised they care they usually don't take prisoners." The men laughed at my half-hearted joke, but it made me wonder why I was still alive. I killed five of them before my gun jammed and another with my knife before they knocked me out. They should have killed me on the spot.

It took another week to reach Kras. We weren't treated kindly. Kras was dug into the side of an asteroid with artificial life support in the compound. Everything was metal and unnerved most men. To me, it was home. Most of my adult life was spent on a ship. Granted the accommodations would not be as nice as what the army provided. It wouldn't matter though if the guards didn't pay attention I'd be dead soon. I kept a wary eye out as Kelsairan prisoners watched me pass.

We were taken to a set of holding cells and kept in a group of four. For the moment we remained together. It was good news for me; I might make it to breakfast after all. Four mattresses lined the floor with a communal toilet in the center. A single yellow bulb lit the room, and the thick metal door had only a slit for a window. Thank God I'm not claustrophobic.

That night I lay in bed staring at the door uncomfortable in the new surroundings. Something was wrong; I could feel it. A shadow passed over the window. The prison was supposed to be on lockdown until the morning. Guards would have turned the lights on by now. I kicked Dan sleeping on the mattress at my feet and threw my shirt at Jim. I hushed them before either spoke. Jim kicked Steve awake, and we all huddled in the corner waiting for whatever came through the door.

My heart pounded in my chest as I waited. I licked my lips as I stared at the door. Two Kelsairans by the look of them slipped into our cell. All four of us rushed them taking advantage of the dark. I'm still not sure of what happened. I do know that one of the Kelsairans had a knife and managed to stab Steve. Jim and Dan wrestled the other to the floor leaving me alone with the second. One Kelsairan against one human wasn't fair by any means. Kelsairan males were twice as strong as human males and very fast. Their females were only slightly less formidable. Luckily I had my military training to fall back on, and this Kelsairan was not military as well. I managed to knock him out just as guards came running.

The light was thrown on, and I was hit on the back of the head. My vision blurred but I didn't pass out. They rolled me off the Kelsairan and stared. Stan was drug out, and Dan and Jim were thrown unceremoniously onto their mattresses. I understood very little Kelsairan. From what I did know the guards weren't happy. Whether it was arranged or not at that point I did not know but the Kelsairans were removed, and our door was locked and double checked.

The next morning we were awakened by a dreadful siren that gave me a headache for the rest of the day. We were served some slop before being handed tools and sent to the mines to dig. A guard pulled me out of the pits before lunch, and I was taken to an office of some sort where I was slammed into a chair and told to wait.

A Kelsairan officer entered with a folder under his arm and dismissed the guard. "State your name and rank." He had a translator which meant he needed the information.

"What makes you think I'm military?"

"For one, you single-handedly knocked out a Kelsairan last night and two it says in your processing paperwork that you were picked up on Cemes after a failed reconnaissance mission. So again, please state your name and rank."

"Lieutenant Jackson Peterson, 1651123 United Human Army."

"What were you doing on Cemes?"

"You just told me what I was doing on Cemes."

"Who was your commanding officer?" The officer stared down at me.

"I was," I looked up into opaque, brown eyes.

"Then why were you captured?" He seemed confused by that fact.

"Because I stayed behind to get my men out." I shrugged.

"Do you know Major Trekes?" He paced around the small office.

Trekes, why was he asking me about Trekes? "Everyone knows Trekes."

"I want to know if you know her personally?" He stopped pacing and got in my face.

"Her?" I couldn't help but laugh. The Kelsairans' built Trekes up as a hero. A legendary fighter that most human troops didn't dare say her name. It was considered bad luck. It wasn't that I thought a woman couldn't fight, I was just surprised. When someone said Trekes, an eight-foot-tall Kelsairan man with huge muscles came to mind. "Not a woman," I said the last part out loud without meaning to. The officer didn't take it so well. He beat me pretty severely before calling for his guards. I was taken to the hospital ward if you could call it that. Steve was not there, and I figured that was a bad sign. This man wanted information from me. I hoped it would keep me safe for the moment.

I was in a lot of pain, and the meds the nurse gave me knocked me out. When I woke up, I was worried I'd be stuck in here until that officer got an answer he liked. I didn't know Trekes though. That meant my sentence would be indefinite. My highest priority besides staying alive was learning to speak Kelsairan.

None of the prisoners were going to teach me their language. I would have to learn as I went. I used trying to flirt with the nurse as an excuse. She didn't seem to mind even though she didn't return the favor. She laughed at my feeble attempt and corrected my pronunciations. I must have annoyed her. The nurse kicked me out of the ward a day or two early, in my opinion at least.

Chapter 2

I hoped the fact that I had information would keep me safe. I was wrong. Kelsairans and humans alike started trouble over one matter, or another and I had plenty of opportunities to practice flirting with the nurse. Over the course of five months, though, I began winning more fights than I lost. Even the Kelsairans began leaving me alone. The guards left me alone, too, as long as I never started the fights. They were a lazy lot that acted more like babysitters than guards. The Kelsairan Army official remained absent as well which was fine with me. I didn't expect to get out anytime soon, and I didn't need the kind of trouble he brought.

"Jack, look at the monitors. What's going on? The guards have everyone on." Dan didn't speak Kelsairan. I looked up from my morning slop to the monitors that were usually blank while we ate. It was a Kelsairan news brief. I listened for a moment.

"Something about trying one of their officers. Why do you care about Kelsairan affairs." I was grumpy until I caught the name. "No way."

"Who is it?" Jim wanted to know.

"Trekes."

"But they showed a woman."

"The official said she was a woman," I thought aloud, looking away from the monitor.

"There, they are showing her again."

I looked up and didn't believe my own eyes. I dropped my spoon and got up from my seat. "I can't believe it."

"What's wrong?"

I stared at the screen at the woman I'd met nearly a year ago. "I saved her life." I sank back into my chair and asked them to keep quiet. I'd watch the trial when I could and fill them in at night. But for now, I had to avoid drawing attention. The charges were unbelievable but straightforward 'failure to obey orders.' I watched until they marched us into the mines.

"Is it really Trekes then?" Jim couldn't believe it either.

"Yeah, that's her. Art is apparently short for Artemis." I nearly laughed at the irony of the name she'd adopted; goddess of the hunt indeed.

"What did she do?"

"She refused to fire on a human ship."

"This is *the* Trekes, right?"

"Why do you think the guards had it on all the monitors?" I barely missed a clout on the head from an angry guard. I found my mind drifting back to the first time I met her.

I was on a week leave on Micea. It's a neutral planet, completely alone. It was exactly what I wanted. My tent was pitched, and a fire was blazing. I was a short hike from the lake, perfect for fishing and swimming. I'd been there once before and loved the spot. As I put a pot of coffee on the fire, I saw the ship coming in hot. It was in trouble, and the pilot was struggling to keep it steady. I grabbed my med pack and ran to where it was going to crash.

The ship knocked over trees as it skid into the ground. The earth shook, and there was a crash when it impacted. I nearly lost my footing. It only made me run faster. Whoever it was wouldn't have much time if the ship was heavily damaged. I was relieved to see it was a human craft when I reached the ridge; an old one, but human nonetheless. The hatch was still closed, which was a bad sign; and, the ship was on fire. I found the emergency release lever as I wrapped my hand in the corner of my shirt to protect it from the hot metal. The hatch opened like a charm when I pulled it.

I fell on my ass when I saw an unconscious Kelsairan woman. It was a human craft. Why the hell was a Kelsairan piloting it? She groaned slightly. Kelsairans were the enemy. I should have left her. I couldn't abandon her to die now that I knew she was alive. My honor wouldn't allow it. I cursed the whole time I pulled her out of the wreckage. She was bleeding from a wound in her leg, and I knew my med kit would be useless. Kelsairan anatomy was different than a human's. I cursed again as I hunted for her med kit. Luckily, she'd kept it close at hand, and I found it quickly.

I dragged her to safety just as her ship exploded. It knocked me back a step, and I instinctively covered the woman from debris. The noise had my ears ringing. The heat from the fire was unbearable. I pulled her further away until I could figure out a plan.

It was a long hike back to my camp. I bandaged her wound temporarily before making a sled to take her the rest of the way. Getting her back, unfortunately, was the easy part. I had to properly address the wound on her upper thigh once she was at my camp. Her one-piece outfit complicated everything. I needed to get to the injury, and its location made it impossible to just cut off the pant leg.

My task would have been far easier if Kelsairans didn't look like humans, but they did. They were usually taller and leaner with opaque eyes and ridges on their brows. Everything else made them appear human. This woman was no exception, and she was undeniably attractive. She was tall and slim. Her breasts were small, yet firm; her hips were perfectly curved. She had ice-blonde hair that was slicked back. Her oblong face had high cheekbones and full lips. I was never this close to one of their women before. I never realized how beautiful they were. Well, this one was anyway. I tried waking her first, hoping I wouldn't have to undress her myself but she was unconscious. I considered waiting until morning, but the wound was oozing, and I was afraid of it getting infected.

I shook her one last time before reaching for the zipper at her neck. Nothing, she was out cold. Damn, I pulled the zipper down my hands shaking like I was a virgin. I tried not to look as I quickly undressed her, I put one of my own t-shirts on her, but her body was flawless. If I think about it, I can still remember it now. I draped a blanket over her torso and other leg as I worked on her wound. There was a piece of metal lodged in the wound. I had to fish around for it before disinfecting and bandaging it. She looked ridiculous in my shorts. At least she was dressed.

I didn't want to move her again, so I brought my sleeping bag out of the tent and rolled her in. The coffee I'd started earlier was ruined now. I started a fresh pot for my night vigil. Who was this woman and why was she here? I sank into my chair watching as she slept.

"Jack come on, or the guards'll clobber ya. They called lunch ten minutes ago." It was Jim pulling me out of my thoughts.

"Yeah, all right." I threw down my pickaxe and fell in line. At least I could watch more of the trial.

No such luck the monitors were off as we were marched into the mess hall. I was worried something was going down until I heard the guards talking. The trial was adjourned until tomorrow. So it was back to digging that afternoon.

For some reason, my mind was void of any thought of her except her face as she slept. It was so peaceful and flecked with firelight. How could she be Trekes, how? If I would have left her to die, how many lives would have been spared? Maybe it wasn't her; perhaps I was wrong. How could she be Trekes? My mind played the same questions over and over all afternoon. They haunted me and plagued me, so much so that soon I had a nagging headache. I skipped dinner that evening hoping to be alone.

It was no use. Jim, Dan, and Crow, my cellmates, hounded me for answers. They asked me the same thing I asked myself: "How could you save Trekes?"

"Do you think if I'd known it was Trekes that I would have saved her?" I nearly shouted at them. They stared at one another. "She was a woman, and she was hurt. We were in neutral space. What right did I have to shoot her? How could I have lived with myself if I let her die?"

"He's right," Dan reasoned. He was the oldest, in on a life sentence for crimes none of us knew. He said it was for our protection. Which meant they were pretty bad. Even the Kelsairans avoided him. "We don't know what happened and its best for all of us if it stays that way. No one breathes a word of Jack's involvement with her. Got it?" Jim agreed. I saved his life it was the least he could do for me. Crow was terrified of Dan, so my secret was safe.

I lay in bed that night lost in thoughts of her. I'd hoped I was over all this. I found myself on Micea again as I closed my eyes.

The cool lake breeze blew through the trees as I stared at the foreign stars. The woman sat up with a jolt and said something in Kelsairan. Then, she passed out from the pain. I rearranged the sleeping bag around her before trying to catch a nap in my chair. When I woke again, it was morning, and the fire was nearly out. I built it up and dug out my translator.

She woke again as I made another pot of coffee. "Who are you? What am I doing here?" she demanded.

"My friends call me Jeep. You crash-landed, and I pulled you out." She sat up and fell back in pain. "Lay still I have your med kit, but I can't read Kelsairan I didn't know what to give you." I brought the pack over and showed it to her. She pulled out a syringe and administered a dose of painkiller. She sighed appreciatively before putting it away.

"Why would you save me?"

"Honestly, I thought you were human. Why were you in a human ship?"

"It's a hobby of mine, to fix old crafts whether human or Kelsairan. Obviously, I'm not as good an engineer as I thought."

I couldn't help smiling. "What's your name?"

"Kheda,"

"Kidda," I repeated, and she laughed.

"Kidj-ya," she said more slowly, and I got it right then.

"So what brings you here?"

"Vacation." She looked around. "You, too, I suppose." She sighed and sat up a little. Then, she finally looked at her clothes; my clothes, to be exact. "What is this, what am I wearing? Did you do this?"

"Sorry, you were wounded, I had no choice really." She looked in her shirt and down her legs until she noticed the bandage. I tossed her the shrapnel "I dug that out of your leg last night."

"You didn't... do anything did you?" She was angry and fought to get up.

"No, despite what your government tells you, we humans aren't animals."

"No, but you are a man."

I folded my arms over my chest as I stared down at her. "Not all men are animals, either." She smiled then more at ease. "Come on, you can have my chair for a while." I offered her my arm for support, and she got to her feet. The pain meds were in full effect, and she managed to hobble to my chair. She watched as I heated some of the rations I'd brought in case fishing was bad. She took the bowl of oatmeal questioningly. "It's good for you," I took a bite.

After a few bites, she looked at me. "You're military, aren't you?"

"I am."

"Then Jeep isn't your real name."

"No." I continued to eat. She was worried then, and I should have guessed why sooner. I thought she was the pampered daughter of some official though. I finished my breakfast rather quickly knowing I needed to rest. "I was up most of the night. I need sleep. Will you be all right for a few hours?"

"You trust me?"

"Is there a reason I shouldn't?" She shook her head. I retrieved my sleeping bag and headed for my tent "Oh and Kheda, I sleep with a gun under my pillow." It wasn't just her. I trusted no one and was always ready for a fight.

She was still in my chair when I woke hours later. She was meditating, and I didn't want to disturb her, so I went to the lake to fish. When I came back, she seemed surprised that I'd caught anything. "What's that?"

"Lunch." I showed them to her.

"You eat those?" She wrinkled her nose.

"Of course."

"But they're gross." She waved her hand at the smell.

"Sorry, but I don't have enough rations; this will have to do." She nodded then still skeptical. At least she was willing to give it a try. "I've been thinking, being down a ship poses a problem. My ship is short range only, my unit is supposed to pick me up in a week. I don't think they'll be happy if I bring a Kelsairan on board. But, I can't leave you here. I could take you to a commercial vessel but not dressed like that. Perhaps I could deliver a message to your family, and they could come get you."

"There's no one."

"What do you mean, no one?"

"Are you dumb? I have no family."

Ok, that was a sensitive subject, but I still had no idea how to get her off the planet. We didn't talk the rest of the afternoon. She'd found a book in her medkit and left me in peace. At least I was enjoying part of my vacation. Or was I? I couldn't help but think about her.

We still had plenty of fish for dinner. I began to heat them over the fire as she spoke: "I'm sorry. You didn't know, and I shouldn't have yelled at you." I nodded not knowing what to say. "What about you? Do you have a family?"

I sat down on a log. "My parents are farmers on Sirus Seven. I have a sister, but my kid brother was killed in the war last year."

"Sorry." She looked away.

"I told him not to join the army, but he didn't believe me when I said it wasn't as glorious as the government said it was." I threw a stick in the fire distracting myself. I never liked talking about Seth. "My sister Sarah has twin boys, and I'm hoping to keep them as far away from this as I can."

"What about you? Do you have anyone?" Kheda picked at a string on the shirt she wore.

"Nope; never have time."

"You," too late I'd forgotten she'd said there was no one. She didn't yell though merely shook her head.

"Why'd you join then?" Her brows were scrunched together as she stared at me.

"Hoping to save my friends and family." I wasn't trying to be noble it was the truth. The Sirus system was under constant threat. When they came asking for special recruits to help end that threat I was first in line. It wasn't how I pictured it though I've only been in the Sirus system three times in five years. I still felt I was making a difference and so I stayed in the army. "So, what do you do then besides fixing old ships?"

"Nothing important." She replied, accepting the fish I offered.

We talked until it was time to sleep. I went into my tent leaving Kheda my sleeping bag and the fire. I settled for my cot, pillow, and gun. I fell into an uneasy sleep as if I knew something was wrong.

"Wake up, Jeep. Wake up." Kheda was screaming.

Chapter 3

I sat up in bed; my cell door banged open. It was morning, and I was in Kras. I'd dreamt the whole night of her. God, I thought I was over this. She was on the monitors again now in front of a row of judges all of them asking her questions. Her opaque, blue eyes were full of rage at their accusations. Her short, blonde hair was slicked back neatly. She looked like a caged animal. Every muscle was tense under her one-piece skin-tight black outfit. Her hands were cuffed behind her with a guard to either side. To her credit, she was utterly still despite the pressure.

"What were your orders major?" The official leaned into her face.

"To destroy the human vessel on its way to the Navea system." Kheda's jaw twitched

"Did you do this?" He leaned in closer.

"No sir, I did not." She ground her teeth.

"But those were your orders." He told the room.

"There were civilians on board." Kheda let out a breath as if she were defeated.

"There are never civilians on board military transport vessels." He spat back.

"Perhaps not Kelsairan transports, but on human transports there are." She sounded smug for once. I looked at the monitor shocked. I told her that. "With all due respect sir, I know there were civilians on board." There was a blur in the image, and the court was in turmoil.

"Take the prisoner out. Half hour recess." It was as if something were missing something she said the Kelsairans didn't want anyone to see. What's changed Kheda?, I wondered. I heard the guards talking about her, and none of it was pleasant. I briefly considered knocking their teeth in for suggesting such things about any woman much less her, but I had to lay low. It did give me the idea to pick a fight and lay up in the hospital wing all day to watch the trial.

I found Dan. "Do me a favor; hit me."

"Jack, have you lost it?"

"Do you want to know what's going on with Trekes?"

Dan grinned. "Tomorrow. These Kelsairan trials take the time they'll get to the juicy stuff tomorrow."

I nodded, figuring he was probably right, particularly if she kept making the judges mad. So, it was breakfast and digging like normal.

"Jeep," She'd hobbled to my tent and waited outside wary of the gun I'd warned her about. I unzipped the flap and stared at her. "osimpas wandered through camp we have to get out of here."

"What are osimpas?"

"They feed on plasma packs. They usually stay on the north side of the island. My ship probably drew them. We must leave now."

"They aren't after us. You said so yourself; osimpas feed on plasma packs."

"It's not them that worry me. Cairns hunt them they will hunt us too. We must leave now."

"And go where? I'm sure we can handle a few beasts."

"Cairns are huge beasts and very smart they hunt in packs."

"I've been here before why haven't I seen them?"

"I told you they hunt the osimpas and the osimpas stay north."

"So where do we go?" I was starting to worry because she was worried.

"They can't cross the water." A two-legged creature the size of a medium dog ran past and knocked her off her feet.

"What was that?"

"An osimpa. We must hurry."

"What about my tent? We'll need shelter in case of a storm."

"There is an abandoned base across the lake. We can shelter there." She stood up, and her wound oozed. The creature had caused it to open again when it knocked her down. I picked her up and carried her back to the fire. She collected our med packs should we need them and I ran for my ship. I put her in the other seat and climbed in.

She showed me exactly how to get to the compound and where was the best place to land. I ran her trajectory through in my head and realized this had been her original heading. The signs on the base were Kelsairan. I scrambled out and left her there bleeding and helpless. "You knew this was here. You're military too."

"I am." Her face was expressionless.

"Damn, why didn't you tell me?" My heart started to race as my adrenaline kicked in.

"Would it have made a difference?" She softened slightly

I raised my gun ready to shoot but I couldn't. She could have left me there. She could have taken my ship and let whatever those things were, eat me. "No," I said finally defeated. I put my gun away and picked her up. She showed me the way inside then led me to rooms that she looked to have used before. I set her down on a cot and went back for our med packs. I found her wearing only my shirt and her underwear when I returned to her room. She was tearing my shorts into a bandage. Somehow she couldn't have looked more beautiful than she did at that moment.

"You can't seem to keep your clothes on around me."

"Bring that here." She ignored my comment. I handed her the bag, and she dug around in it for something. She pulled out what looked like a small gun and handed it to me. Then she gave herself a dose of pain meds. "Use it on me."

"What is it?"

"It will bind the flesh."

"Why didn't we do this before?" I was confused.

"Because it was healing on its own." She retorted, then cringed. "and it hurts like hell. Please, I can't see it to do it right. Put the tip in the wound and pull the trigger start at the deepest point and work your way up moving back and forth. Even with the painkiller, I'll probably pass out. Just don't stop. All right?" I nodded then got up to find more lamps. The base still had power at least in this corner.

I still hear her screams sometimes when I'm sleeping. It's no different now, even the hammering of metal on rock can't drown them out. She passed out thankfully after only a few minutes. I wanted a cold beer then, more than I ever had in my life. The flesh was swollen and irritated, so I used what used to be my shorts as a bandage and pulled the cover over her. I found a cot a few doors down and went back to sleep with my gun clutched to my chest.

I woke the next morning to a steaming bowl of stew. Kheda managed to get a food replicator working and wobbled in with it proudly. She was freshly bathed and dressed in a tan t-shirt and pants. Her blonde hair was slicked back and somewhere she'd scrounged up perfume. She smiled knowingly. "I keep a few supplies here in case of trouble. My refuge if you will."

"That's why the base has power?" she nodded. "How's the leg?"

"It will be as good as new soon enough." She moved to leave. "Thank you, Jeep. That's twice you could have done something, and I would have been helpless to stop you."

She left before I could say her thanks was not needed or anything else. After breakfast, I went to the lake to wash up myself. She'd scrounged up clothes for me, and a bar of soap then disappeared. As I stepped into the lake, though, I could feel her watching me.

She came out of the base when I was on the beach with my pants on. "Do you think you could catch some fish for lunch?"

"I thought you said they were gross." She shrugged. I pulled on my shirt and saw her watching me. Huh, wasn't that interesting. She sat by me as I dropped my line in the water. Luckily I kept my pole in my ship.

"What happened to your family, Kheda?"

"I renounced them when I joined the army."

"Why would you do that?"

"All of us do. We fight for our families, but they cannot be held accountable for our actions in war."

"Held accountable by whom?"

"Our god."

I was astounded but didn't dare question her belief system. I'm sure mine would seem just as crazy to her. "Is that why there is no man in your life?"

"Women in service to their people are not allowed to marry. It is too hard to face the enemy if you are worried who will care for your children." She told me.

"Isn't it the same for the men though?"

"Women raise the children on Kelsair."

"Why did you join then?" I was confused. Why would any woman want to join their army?

"To save my brother. On Kelsair, one child from every house must serve their people. My brother was a gentle soul a singer and poet. This life was not meant for him." She shrugged.

"Why do you speak of him in the past tense?"

"He is dead to me."

"But he's still alive?"

"A very successful singer. Somehow I inherited everything he did not. Tell me about you humans. You said you simply had no time. Could you marry if you wanted?"

"Of course I could. As a matter of fact, many of the men and women in the army are married. They travel from base to base with their spouse, so they're never far apart. It certainly makes the transport vessels less lonely."

"There are civilians on transport vessels? Why would you do that?"

"To transport people." I was confused. I knew the Kelsairans attacked transports, but it seemed they didn't know the truth in what they were doing. "You didn't know, did you?"

"No, you must stop your people from doing that."

"They don't do it often, but sometimes they have to. Try scanning for civilians next time." My line caught then, and she helped me reel in lunch.

"It's my fault." I gasped.

"Jack, you all right?" Jim was concerned.

I leaned in close "She's on trial because of something I told her."

"Then you saved innocent people." Dan clapped me on the back. "Time for lunch. They called it early so they could get back to the trial." I nodded numbly.

There she was on the monitors again; her demeanor had not changed. The hard edge of Trekes was present and not the softer Kheda I met. "There was another instance when you did not fire on an enemy ship was there not Major Trekes?"

"There was." The room gasped. How could they know these things about her?

"On day 127 in the year of Laman, you and your squadron were engaged in a firefight with a squadron of human vessels. Is that correct?" The official paced in front of her.

"Yes," Kheda said coldly.

"You destroyed how many ships that day, major?"

"Five." Her voice was hard and distant.

"Can you speak up?" He stopped pacing to face the room.

"Five, sir." She said pointedly.

"And yet you merely took out the engines of the sixth. Curious, I took the liberty of checking your ships logs and do you know what I found major?" He leaned on the railing near her.

"Yes."

"Please tell the court what I found." He addressed Kheda.

"I was scanning the beacons of the ship before engaging them." She took a deep breath and let it out.

"And why exactly were you doing this?"

"Because I owed a human my life." The room gasped again. "The pilot of the sixth vessel was the man that saved my life when my ship went down on Micea nearly a year ago. Without his help, I would be dead now. I owed him my life my debt is now repaid."

"Can you prove your story?" He raised his brows.

"I only have a scar on my leg and his beacon number to prove my claim." Kheda raised her chin.

"And his name?" The official started pacing again.

"He said his name was Jeep." Kheda's eye twinkled as her lip quirked up at the corner.

"Jeep? What kind of name is that?" He stopped pacing to stare at her.

She smiled and repeated exactly what I'd told her when she'd asked the same question "A twentieth-century earth conveyance. Sir."

"She makes a mockery of this court remove her." The center judge shouted. That's the Kheda I knew.

"Your honor tomorrow I wish to call into evidence more on this line. If the judges will humor me, I intend to prove that Major Trekes is under the influence of this human." It had to be her lawyer if Kelsair had such a thing.

"Try what you want she's not the same Trekes she was. The court is adjourned." The center judged heaved a sigh.

The monitors were black again, and I hurriedly told Dan and Jim what happened. "What did you do to her?" Dan was shocked.

"I was a perfect gentleman," I swore.

"Maybe she's not used to that in the Kelsairan army," Dan suggested.

"Do me a favor find out what you can about her from the Kelsairans." Dan looked at me. "None of us knew Trekes was a woman till all this started." Dan nodded.

I spent the entire afternoon discreetly gathering information from anyone I could. "What's really going on with Trekes? Everything they tell us humans is to make our knees shake."

The Kelsairan stared at me. No one knew his real name, so we all called him M. "What's it to you, Jack?"

"The way I see it she keeps up the way she's going, and she's headed here." I moved closer talking low so the guards wouldn't hear.

M stared again. "Looking to boost your rep? The nurse ain't good enough for you anymore?"

"Wrong rep, M."

"Ah, want to take on Trekes the badest of the bad." He nearly laughed at me.

"Only if she's everything they say she is."

"Oh, she is. I wouldn't try it if I were you though. She'd eat you for breakfast then have you for dessert if you get my drift."

"Are you saying what I think you're saying?"

"Oh, the major knew how to have a good time."

"Then maybe I can kill two birds with one stone."

I said walking away cringing at what I'd just said: "You're asking for trouble Jack." The other conversations I had were similar to the one with M. She had a reputation among the Kelsairans. She was a charismatic leader to her men. They idolized her but feared her at the same time. She'd run into a firefight to save any of them and took several of her own men to her bed. It just didn't make sense. At first, I thought it started after I'd met her, but it seemed to be a long-standing tradition. Almost a right of passage in her unit, something was wrong. Dan told me the same news and looked just as confused. He wasn't a soldier, but he knew behavior like that would never be tolerated in the human army.

Dan and I worked out a plan to get me to the hospital ward the next day and not get me killed in the process. I told Dan what M said about the nurse and me, and he merely laughed. Then he looked at me quite seriously and asked if it were true. I told him then about the nurse and one of the guards, she'd merely been an excuse to learn the language, but the prisoners could talk all they wanted.

I had nightmares that night about Kheda and her men. Things I never wanted think about her, things I refused to believe. Then my dreams turned more severe, and I began to dread the fight Dan, and I had planned. Why was I doing this? I was awake before the siren and Dan gave me a nod as he pulled on his shirt. I'd pick a fight in line for breakfast.

Chapter 4

Here we go, I sighed to myself as I knocked Dan's tray out of his hand. He yelled at me and took a swing. I ducked to make it look good and landed a punch in his gut. He decked me, and I acted like it was a lucky shot, and I was out cold. It was quick enough to keep the guard's wrath off Dan and enough to land me in the hospital ward at least for the morning.

Teesa was at my bed when I pretended to come to. Her ministrations were always welcome, no matter if they were needed or not. The monitors were off, but Teesa was already glancing at the door. I caught her on the right day. "You could leave the monitor on to keep me company if you have work to do Teesa."

"You're feeling better then, Jack?" Tesa checked my vitals and smiled at me.

"I always do under your care," I assured her.

"All right; I'll turn them on and check on you soon." She hurried off.

Teesa was true to her word. The monitor was turned on, and she left me completely alone. Trekes was led into the courtroom in chains. Today she wore blue instead of her usual drastic black. But the one piece suit was just as skin tight and no less revealing. She faced the judges proud as always as her lawyer began to speak.

"If it pleases the tribunal, I intend to show that Major Trekes is still loyal to her people. She was merely under the influence of this human she felt she owed her life to."

"A supposed human; there is no proof he exists." The court's official pointed out to the room.

"I have evidence to support her claims." The man squirmed before the judges. He seemed small for a Kelsairan. "The major submitted to a physical by the jail nurse last night and I have her findings here." He held up the report and handed it off to a court runner.

The center judge looked it over. "Let the records indicate that the nurse found a six-inch scar on the major's upper inner thigh with traces of shrapnel healed with a tissue fuser from any medical pack." He looked to Kheda's representative. "It proves she was injured."

"The nurse is willing to testify that a wound such as the major's could not have been healed by her own hand. The angle was wrong, and she would have passed out from the pain before she finished the procedure."

"I still don't see the relevance," another judge began. The center judge cut him off.

"Proceed, but you'll need more concrete evidence than a medical report and speculation." He sat back in his chair rubbing his chin.

"We have a bio signature from the base. It's not enough for positive identification of the specific human, but it was enough to prove there was a human on the base." Trekes grinned. She was an engineer if she wanted the bio signature read accurately it would have been. She was protecting my identity. I couldn't imagine why though. The lawyer handed over the chip, and it was displayed for the whole court. Two biosignatures coming in and out of the compound for days one Kelsairan female and one human male.

"Her biosignature can't be read either." The judge pointed out.

"No, but her beacon and radio transmissions place her on the planet during this time period. Not to mention she booked passage on a commercial ship back to Kelsair after the last bio signature is gone. We have the record here."

The judge nodded finally as he sat straight once more. "All right; we'll hear her story."

Artemis was lead forward and her chains removed for the first time I remembered seeing. She addressed each of the judges by name and thanked them for the opportunity to speak on her own behalf. The center judge waved it off, "Tell us what happened major."

"I had two weeks leave and decided to spend it on Micea. I took an old human cruiser which I'd rebuilt. It's a hobby of mine rebuilding old ships. The trip was uneventful until I entered the atmosphere. Then I lost an engine, and the cabin caught fire. I managed to put the fire out, by then I was dangerously low, and it was a difficult landing. I was knocked unconscious. I would be dead, if not for Jeep."

"And this human simply saved your life?"

"He did. He admitted to me later that he thought I would be human because of my ship yet couldn't leave me to die."

"Tell us what happened then."

She told them an abbreviated version of the five days we spent together. She told them about the osimpas and the cairns and how I got her across the lake to the base. Then she explained to them how she'd asked me to heal her wound and how reluctant I was to inflict such pain on her. That part they didn't quite believe. She made the rest up, though. She told them we spent our remaining days together in silence talking to each other only at meal times and that I agreed to take her to the trade route so I wouldn't feel guilty about leaving her behind. She told them about our deal with the beacon her way of repaying her debt. She said we both tried to get military information out of the other once we figured out we were both in the army. She managed to convince them that it was then that I'd told her about the civilians on the transports.

They bought the story hook line and sinker. Kheada must have been practicing it all week if not from the moment she was put in chains. I had no clue what would happen from here. The center judge called a recess to allow them to gather their questions. I looked up and noticed Tessa hovering in the door. The monitor went black. "You need to rest now, Jack."

"Teesa, I'm fine."

"Now Jack, don't give me any trouble." She gave me an injection, and I was out before I could object.

I came to hours later as I was being hauled to my feet "Damn, Tessa." I grumbled and received an angry smack on the back of my head. I looked over at the culprit. "Sorry, Salea. did she really have to knock me out though?" Salea was Teesa's lover.

"You were supposed to be in need of medical attention remember Jack?" he looked at me as he made sure I was steady on my feet. "Why were you so interested in the trial anyway? It was a Kelsairan affair."

"Is it over?"

"Sentenced her while you slept." Salea looked at me from the corner of his eye.

"Where's she headed?" I tried to act uninterested.

"What's this about?" He stopped walking.

"The major and I have a score to settle if she's headed this way I want first crack at her." I balled up my fists trying to be angry.

"Were you in the army Jack?" Salea's shoulders sagged. He and I actually got along.

"My brother was." He bought it.

"Then you'll be disappointed she's going to Rotea. The judges are convinced she can be rehabilitated. What a shock, especially after it came out that she and that human had an affair. I thought she was headed here for sure." An affair? I was blown away she and I hadn't done anything. I didn't show my shock though I had to get Salea to commit just in case plans changed.

"But if she does come I get first crack at her right Salea?" I asked.

"Jack, I can't promise." He shook his head.

I pulled him in close. "Right now everyone knows Teesa is having an affair, but they think it's with me. Somehow in your twisted

Kelsairan culture, that's all right. I'd hate to see what happens if they found out what's really going on."

"You wouldn't." Salea was shocked I would stoop so low.

"Try me." I dared him.

"All right Jack, on one condition. Get Dan to beat you up in three days just like today." I grinned at him. Relationships between and men and women really didn't change no matter what race. I nodded my agreement, and he took me back to my cell.

Dan, Jim, and Crowe were waiting for me. They pulled me to the far corner to talk as soon as the cell door was closed. "Why didn't you tell us?" Jim asked.

"It never happened," I assured them.

"They had it on tape." I stared at Dan dumbfounded. "You didn't see it? What happened to our plan then?"

"Teesa knocked me out all afternoon."

"It was blurred, but it looked like her." Crow offered.

"Well, it wasn't me." I got up and paced a moment before returning to them "did the coverage of the trial seem to jump?"

"It did," Dan replied. "I noticed it did the same thing a few days ago."

"Then, at her sentencing, she had on different clothes, almost like it was the next day."

"They edited her trial. There's something they didn't want anyone to see." I heaved a sigh. "What does it matter it's over now she's going to Roteo."

"She'll escape from Roteo," Dan commented.

"Not if she wants her career."

"If they're editing her trial she may not have one. I say she's coming here." Dan replied.

I nodded. "Then you'll beat me up again?" Dan stared at me as if I were crazy.

I hardly slept that night. I thought about her all night and the way we really spent our days together.

"You know, Jeep, I'd hate to ruin both our vacations. We could spend them together. What I mean is you could drop me off just before meeting up with your ship."

"Then what will we do for three days?"

"You could teach me to fish." She offered. I knew the situation was dangerous. Not the kind of danger you face in combat but the kind that comes in relationships. She was so close as I handed her my pole I could smell her perfume. The sun in her blonde hair and the way the breeze pushed it into her eyes; I should have been more careful. But I think by then it was too late. I helped her reel in another fish and showed her how to bait the hook. She was the first woman I'd met that wasn't squeamish about it.

We spent all afternoon fishing and talking. Kheda told me about Kelsair, and I told her about Sirus Seven. It was as if here on Micea the war didn't exist, and we weren't soldiers fighting for opposite sides. I showed her how to clean the fish but wouldn't let her do it. It was for selfish reasons really; I just didn't want her to smell like them. I went for a quick swim in the lake trying to wash the smell away, but she still complained. It didn't keep her from sitting close though.

That evening, we walked the perimeter of the entire island. She pointed out the stars she knew, and I merely listened. I couldn't help but notice she slowed her pace as we neared the base. I matched it not in a hurry to go in either. But once we were there we went into our own rooms. My gun went back under its pillow that night.

The next day was spent almost the same way. I couldn't help noticing how quickly her leg was healing. We could walk further now and ventured into the jungle behind the base. She led me to a waterfall and a small pool, where I discovered she didn't know how to swim. As a matter of fact, she seemed petrified of the water. After much convincing, she finally got in. It took most of the afternoon, but she eventually got the hang of it. We took another walk around the island that night talking about trivial things. Somewhere along the way, her hand found its way into mine.

I went to my room at the base wishing things could be different. Wishing the war didn't exist and that Khedae was not the enemy. I turned when I heard the door open, and there she was looking ridiculous in my t-shirt. "I just wanted to say thank you for teaching me to swim. I've been scared of the water since I was little. But I'm not scared anymore."

"I'm glad, Kheda."

"Jeep I..." I could see it in her eyes she wanted to say everything that I was thinking. "goodnight." I crossed the room without thinking and kissed her. She melted in my arms a moment before pulling away. "We can't," she didn't give me a reason, and she didn't need to there were a thousand of them hanging over our heads.

"Goodnight then," I said expecting her to leave.

"Could I, would you hold me tonight, please." We both wanted so much more, but we had to settle for that small consolation. I climbed into bed and set my gun on the floor under it. "You weren't kidding then?" she eyed over the gun.

"Don't take offense, old habits die hard." I moved over, and she climbed in beside me. I wrapped my arms around her hoping I'd never have to let go. I didn't think either of us would get much sleep that night crowded in that small bed, but we both slept more soundly than we had in years.

Kheda was at the foot of the bed meditating when I woke the next morning. I watched her for a short time until she opened her eyes. She smiled at me then went for breakfast. I was dressed by the time she came back. "We should head over to the other island and pack up my camp. Then check out your ship and see if there's anything worth saving." She nodded.

"It should be safe but take your gun just to be sure."

We said very little to each other that day. It was as if it would break the spell of the last few days. In the morning I would take her to a trade ship where she could buy passage home. And I would meet up with my ship. We would be enemies again and would never see one another.

Kheda's ship was a total loss. There was one strong box that made it with her money ID and gun. Had I cared I could have found out who she was then. To me, she was merely Kheda and to be painfully honest, I really didn't want to know. She could have found out who I was just as easily, but she didn't seem to want to know either. I suppose, for us, it was better that way.

Once my ship was packed we headed back to the base and hiked back up to the waterfall for a swim. We still talked very little it was enough just to be near one another. Nightfall came all too quickly as we hiked back to base and soon her hand found mine again. Her perfume still lingered despite the swim and wafted on the breeze. We sat on the bank of the lake not wanting to sleep but it was getting late, and we couldn't afford to oversleep.

I went to my room, and she followed me in. Kheda kissed me goodnight, and I longed for more. Her hands wandered, and so did mine but just as suddenly as it started, it stopped. "I can't, I'm sorry."

I pulled her close. "You have nothing to be sorry for." I was confused. Yesterday it was we, and today it was I. Something had changed in her thinking and I doubted she would tell me what it was. She pulled away to leave. "Please, Kheda, stay like last night. I won't do anything else, I swear to you." She nodded. I pulled off my shirt, and she reached for it. I handed it over and looked away as she changed. I shook my head knowing I'd never look at my t-shirts without thinking of her. I climbed into bed, and she lay down beside me.

"We will be enemies again tomorrow," Kheda said quietly as she played with my hand that was draped over her chest. "I can't bear the thought of killing you."

"That certainly makes me feel better." I smiled even though I knew she was trying to be serious.

"Jeep, please; we are soldiers. We have a duty to our people. We can't quit simply because we met, yet I could not kill you." She sat up and looked down at me.

"So what do you suggest?" I ran the back of my fingers over her cheek.

Kheda leaned into my touch. "A truce between the two of us; I will give you my beacon code, and you will give me yours. Neither will fire on the other."

"That's a dangerous game, Kheda." I pulled her to my chest kissing the top of her head.

She looked up at me. "I'm willing to take the risk."

"And somehow you already knew I would be willing to." I sighed. "Why do we have to be at war?"

"Do not wish for what cannot be. This is all I can give you." I nodded and told her my beacon code. She repeated it over and over before saying hers. I fell asleep with those numbers rolling through my head.

Chapter 5

The next morning was one of the hardest of my life watching her disappear into the crowd of the trade station as if she loathed me. I knew she was doing it to save my life, but it didn't keep it from hurting. I'd never see her again, and I didn't get to kiss her goodbye. That was it she was simply gone.

"Jack, wake up. How can you sleep through the siren?" Dan was punching my arm.

"Damn," I got out of bed to return to the monotony my life had become. The next two weeks were like nothing ever happened. No trial and no Trekes. It was mining, fighting and maneuvering with the guards. God, how I loathed my life. I suddenly longed to be back on a battlefield or in a dogfight anything to break up the mundane.

Then, one afternoon I got my wish. Salea found me just as I was getting into line to head back to the mine. He yanked me hard by the arm and nearly threw me the opposite direction. Dan gave him a hard look, and I shook my head. I had a feeling something was going down.

"Move it," Salea pushed me forward.

"Where are we going?" I looked back at him.

"You wanted your shot? Well, you'll get it soon enough." So I was right they were sending her here after all. How the hell was I going to make this look believable and not get either of us hurt in the process? I was worried now. For weeks I'd been convinced she was on her way to Roteo and now I had maybe an hour to think.

Salea stopped in front of a large workout room that was rarely used and opened the door. Six other men were already inside. I stared at him fuming. "It's this or nothing."

I stepped inside, and he shut the door. This was bad. There were four humans and two Kelsairans. The humans were thugs, only one of them would offer me a challenge. I knew the two Kelsairans though. I avoided them at all costs apart they weren't so bad, but they were always together. Dan and I could handle one, but I wasn't sure if Kheda could handle both of them and the other four. I didn't know if I would have the opportunity to help her. I scanned the room looking for cameras. Three of them were on. Whatever I did, it had to look like it was for selfish reasons if I was going to be any help to her after this.

The seven of us stared at one another as we waited. It didn't bother me, it actually bought me the time I needed to think. I found a seat in the corner and crossed my arms. "Should have known you would show up, Jack." One of the Kelsairans moved closer. "M says you asked about her weeks ago."

"Won't Teesa be mad?" the other chimed in.

"One way or another she's just another Kelsairan." They were trying to goad me into a fight hoping to knock out their competition.

"Want to know what your problem is, Jack?" One Kelsairan started, "You don't know where you belong." The other finished.

"I certainly don't belong with that rabble." Both of them smirked and backed off. It was hard to fight with someone if you found them amusing. They moved back towards the door when footsteps came down the hall, but I stayed right where I was. The lights went out, and the door flew open. They were at least going to give her a fighting chance.

The four humans attacked like a pack of dogs when the lights came on. She punched one in the face, kicked another in the chest and punched another in the ribs. Then she dropped and swept the fourth's legs. The Kelsairans seemed like they were going to hang back, but when they saw what she did to the humans, they joined in. She grabbed one of their arms and broke it with a resounding crack. Then she moved him in front of his own friend to block a punch. As the second Kelsairan pulled back to punch again, she kicked him faster than I thought even a Kelsairan was capable.

Two of the humans were back on their feet now and more wary of her. She broke one of the human's legs with a swift kick to the shin. He went down which left the two Kelsairans and one human. She kicked the Kelsairan with two working arms in the groin and finished him off with a kick to the jaw. The last human swung at her, and she batted him away focusing on the Kelsairan. I used the opportunity to move in closer. The Kelsairan kicked at her, and she caught his leg. She backhanded him with her free fist and brought her elbow down on his leg dislocating his knee. He collapsed out cold.

She turned looking for the last human, but he was gone. I knocked him out while she was preoccupied. I moved in fast and tackled her to the ground before she could attack me. She fought me with every ounce of strength she had and nearly knocked me off. I smacked her or at least pretended to for the cameras. That surprised her more than anything else.

"Kheda it's me just pretend to fight," I whispered so only she would hear. She punched me for real and my vision blurred. I pinned her down and lay on top of her. I recited her beacon code in her ear, and she stopped fighting.

"Jeep, how the hell did you get here?"

"It's a long story, and for now we have to make this look good, or you'll be a target for a lot more attacks." She glanced to the cameras as I moved both her wrists into one hand.

"Surely the guards..."

"Who do you think set this up?" She tried to roll me, and I banged her head on the ground or at least made it look like I did. She lay there as if dazed. "You're in trouble, like it or not, and you need my help." She fought again, and I acted as though I banged her head on the ground.

I pulled the zipper on her one piece "Jeep please," she begged me.

"I won't do anything, I swear; but, they have to think I did. I'm sorry. And you can't call me that here. My name is Jackson, but they all call me Jack." She nodded, and a tear rolled down her cheek. "The cameras won't see anything," I unzipped it further and slid my hand inside. She feigned one last attempt at a struggle and I, the villain, knocked her out. She lay there a moment as I pulled her clothes down cursing myself. Then, thankfully, they shut off the lights.

It was pitch black and safe to move. I helped Kheda dress, then stumbled with her to the corner. I sat down next to her and whispered sorry in her ear once again. She took my hand in hers and sat there in silence for a long time. I told her the lights would come on soon, and they'd take her away. Then I got up to lean against the wall hoping to look like I was gloating.

I expected to see her curled into a ball when the lights came on. Instead, she staggered to her feet and waited for the guards. They arrived only moments later and grabbed her by the arms. I thanked god Salea was with them, he at least could be trusted. She leaned on a guard, acting as though I'd hurt her but kicked one of the men on the ground on the way out. They told me to go to dinner as they began pulling men out.

"What went down this afternoon?" Dan asked as I sat down across from him.

"She's here," Dan stared at me. "I had some dirt on one of the guards, and he arranged a meeting. It was supposed to be in private but..." I shrugged.

"I'm sure we'll hear about it soon enough then." Dan leaned in.

"I'm anxious to hear what they say as well." I looked to Dan "She took out six men including two Kelsairans."

"And we wondered how she earned her reputation."

"My idea won't last long. We have to get out of here, or they'll kill her or worse." I whispered to Dan.

"Have you lost it? We're on Kras. There's no getting out." His reply was urgent but just as discreet.

"Want to come with me."

Dan grinned. "You bet your life I do."

That night I was restless. I was worried about where they'd taken Kheda. I was cursing myself for what I had done. What if all I had accomplished was to show someone else how to take advantage of her? My mind was racing, and the siren was blaring before I realized it. It was time to face another day.

I went to breakfast like usual, and she was nowhere to be seen. I sat down across from Dan as the line died away. Halfway through the slop, they fed us, the room fell silent as she strode into the room. She was dressed in a black t-shirt and black pants. Her prison-issued boots looked two sizes too big, but I didn't think that would make her any less efficient at killing anyone. She went through the breakfast line ignoring the catcalls and snide comments. One man spit on her, and she backhanded him. He lost a tooth, and she never looked up from her tray. At the end of the line, she looked up at the sea of men.

"Major," I called and stood up. God, what was I thinking? I pointed to the empty chair beside mine, and the room buzzed. I sat back down and waited. She came over with a sneer and sat down. It was the same look of contempt she'd had when she disappeared into the crowd on the trade ship.

"Jack," she spat.

"Where'd they take you?" I asked quietly.

"Solitary."

"Eat quickly they'll take us to the mines soon."

"I'm going to the hospital ward. I have to work there two days a week." She whispered as she scanned the room.

I nodded and noticed the guards waiting for her. "Don't let any of the guards get you alone."

"Teesa's already told me which can be trusted." Good old Teesa, but oh was she going to be furious with me.

I looked up and notice Jim staring at her. "That's Jim, Dan, and Crow. My cellmates; we stick together for safety." She nodded before glancing up at the guards.

She got up without finishing her breakfast. "Don't wear yourself out in the mine. I'd hate for you to be too tired to put up a fight." Dan watched her leave as did half the room. The other half was staring at me. This wasn't what I had planned.

The entire day in the mines, I heard rumors all of them untrue. Some were about what happened last night others were about my non-existent relationship with Trekes. I was humiliating the one woman I ever cared about all in the hope of protecting her and I had a sinking feeling it wasn't going to work. I needed to speak with her but how was I ever going to find the privacy.

I went to my cell that night after I didn't find her at dinner. Dan, Jim, and Crow were still in the mess hall playing dice. I don't know what they were playing for, but they seemed to be having a good time. I sat down on my bunk and put my head in my hands. As if I conjured her into being she appeared in my door. I looked up surprised. She shut the door and crossed the room.

I grabbed her roughly fearing she was a dream. Her arms slid around me, and she lay her head on my shoulder. "You brilliant man."

"What? What are you talking about?"

"You unwittingly made them think we are in a tratari relationship."

"I don't know what that is." I looked at her confused.

"One where you must earn the right to take me."

"That certainly explains your comment, but I don't like it. What if someone else gets the same idea?"

"It's not that simple. I get a say in it too, and after I took down six men well, this at least will buy us time."

"I spent all day fearing what you'd say to me." She smiled up at me. "Kheda I,"

"You can't call me that either. No one is supposed to know that name. It died the day I joined the army."

I nodded. "We have to find a way to escape."

"I'm one step ahead of you. There is a way just give me time. I know a few people here." I looked at her. "You're not in my position without making allies along the way." She pulled me to the bed and sat down.

"Jack, I was set up. Parts of my trial were edited. They did not want me to escape because I said and did things I shouldn't. If you leave with me, it could be dangerous."

"I don't care, Artemis," I replied. She looked disappointed with the name. Kheda kissed me gently anyway.

"I don't like the beard." She replied.

"It has to stay for now." She smacked me hard across the mouth and split my lip. "What was that for?" I asked.

"Sorry, but it has to look believable I do have a reputation to uphold." Her lip twitched up at the corner. I sighed. "Hit me." She ordered.

"I can't," I shook my head.

"Jack," she said exasperated "Bite me." She tried instead.

"Kinky, can we do this some other time for real." She smiled at me then. I took off my shirt and handed it to her. She took it happily and changed as I pulled off my boots.

"I do like the muscles," she commented as she climbed into bed beside me.

"Six months of digging in the mines and getting my ass kicked by Kelsairans." I huffed.

"Surely you beat them sometimes." Her brows drew together as she stared at me.

"I'm getting better at it." I admitted, "Was Teesa mad at me?"

"Teesa? What do you care about her?" She was jealous. I could tell by the tone in her voice.

"She was one of my only friends in here that's all."

She looked up at me "Then no, she is one of my friends. I knew her before I came. Lucky for us, any other nurse would have found out what didn't happen."

She stretched out alongside me, and I pulled her close. I bit her neck just where it met her shoulder. She complained but didn't struggle. I let go and changed my grip a little just to make it look like she did. When I was done, she had a large bruise on her neck. She rolled over and kissed me again. She said goodnight and settled into sleep. I knew we both wanted more but the thought of my first time with her here in this disgusting filthy jail cell didn't seem fitting, so I lay on my back and slowed my breathing waiting for sleep to come.

Dan woke us before the siren the following day. He seemed happy to catch us together. "I don't know what really went down in that room, but five different stories are floating around. And you, young lady, better watch out for those two Kelsairans you beat the shit out of. They're out for blood now."

"Doesn't seem to have changed my situation much." Kheda shrugged.

"Well, at least it looks like your scheme will work for the most part but whatever you're planning you'd better do it quickly," Dan advised. "Jack you better watch your back. There's a lot of men in here that don't like the way things went down."

"Or that I've made one of their decorated officers my lap dog, I'll be careful." I found Kheda's clothes and handed them back to her. She slinked into her pants then turned her back to change her shirt. She handed me back my t-shirt, and I frowned "You gave the last one back with your perfume on it."

"And I bet you still have it," she whispered in reply.

"Still neatly folded in my footlocker." She pulled on her boots with a smile. The sirens blared, and our door flew open. Dan left, and Jim and Crow were just getting up. "When did you learn English?"

"After our encounter. When did you learn Kelsairan?"

"After an army official came to question me about you." She looked at me surprised. "I'll tell you later." She nodded as she watched me put on my boots.

Chapter 6

We had the same routine for three weeks, and we were no closer to an escape plan. Then, one morning, she made a giant show of ignoring me. I was at a loss. Our whole strategy could fall to pieces if she kept this up but I couldn't figure out what was going on. She went to breakfast alone and sat by herself. I said something to her and even moved to hit her, but she merely blocked. I left it alone then hoping whatever was going on would pass.

She found Salea after she finished eating, but it wasn't her day to work in the hospital ward. I was concerned for a moment that Salea had double-crossed me then cursed myself. She was a woman, Kelsairan anatomy was like human anatomy it was probably just time for her courses. And from what she'd said about the type of relationship we were supposed to be in it certainly explained her behavior. I heaved a silent sigh of relief.

Three days later, I said good morning, and she smacked me so hard that I nearly fell out of my chair. She set down her tray and moved to sit down beside me. I grabbed her wrist and twisted it behind her back until she bent down to my eye level. I snatched a kiss, and the Kelsairans laughed as I let her go. She sunk into her seat sulking. "Feeling better?"

"My problems as a female are not your concern." She confirmed my suspicions.

Things were back to normal that day, but she made sure we snuck away from dinner early. She checked up and down the hall for guards as she slipped into my room. "I have a plan, but you have to actually hit me this time. I need an excuse to get out of the mines tomorrow."

"What are you up to?"

"Scouting. I dare not say too much you never know who's listening."

"Artemis, I can't hit you."

"Just a couple where they can see them, you must. I hit you."

"Yes, I noticed. Didn't you ever learn to pretend? You hit really hard."

"But you're so cute when you go all bleary-eyed." She teased.

"That's really not funny."

"But I hit you all the time. I humiliate you in front of all those men." She was trying to work me up so I would hit her anyway.

"It won't work Artemis. I know why you did it and I could see that you hated doing it. You can hide it from them but not from me." I sighed. "Is this really necessary?"

She nodded. "I want it to look like you were so happy to have me back that I can hardly walk."

"We really have a weird relationship; you know that, right?"

"Jack I..."

"Just don't look, God, I can't believe I'm doing this." I smacked her as hard as I could knocking her to the ground. She got up, and I punched her in the jaw not as hard, but enough to leave a good bruise. Then I wrapped my hands around her throat avoiding her windpipe and squeezed just hard enough for another set of bruises. I can't imagine the amount of trust she placed in me to let me do such things, but the most confusing was how I earned it. I nearly cried when I saw a tear roll down her cheek. Just one tear was all that escaped, and it had nothing to do with physical pain. "Let's call it an early night," I said my voice shaking.

"Wait," She hit me square in the eye but not as hard as she usually would have. Then she scratched my neck and down my chest with her nails. Somehow it made me feel better, but she looked just as upset as I felt.

"The sooner we get out of here, the better. I can't take much more of this."

"I think I'd rather let them have me than keep this up."

I turned abruptly realizing she was serious. "Don't give up; we'll get out. Do whatever it is that you're planning tomorrow and we'll go from there, all right? I can't lose you again Kheda." I whispered in her ear. She kissed me long and hard, but I pulled away. "Let's go to sleep." There was a reason we hadn't done anything on Micea. Nothing that involved the war or even the fact that we were two different races. It was something with her, and I wasn't going to let her go back on whatever that was now. Not like this. I'd be prepared, too, whenever she was ready.

She said nothing for a week about her scouting expedition. For a while, I was beginning to think it was a wash. Then, one night, she pulled me away from dinner early. I was afraid she was going to try another crazy scheme like last week but she led me to the hospital wing. We made it through the corridors which wasn't hard at this time of night. The guards were sure the prison was escape-proof. As long as the prisoners were under control and in reasonable numbers, they could go almost anywhere they wanted in the evening. There were cameras everywhere, and it made the guards even lazier.

We went into Teesa's office which I'd never been in before. She pointed under the desk, and I crawled in. She locked the door and opened a drawer before meeting me under the desk. "What's this all about?"

"There are no cameras in here, and she has a signal scrambler in case of bugs in her office."

"Then why are we under the desk?" I frowned at her.

"The door has a window. I locked the outer door, too, but I didn't want to take any chances. I found our way out." She glanced up at the ceiling then around the edge of the desk.

"So it was worth all the snide comments?" I asked running a hand over the scratches she gave me.

"Stop joking Jack." She smacked my arm and frowned.

"All right what's the plan?"

"We steal the supply ship," Kheda said quickly.

"I think they've thought of that." I thought she was crazy.

"They have but only after it's unloaded." She explained. I was curious now. "Stowing away in their excess cargo won't get us anywhere they check for that and we won't have control of the ship. And stealing the ship once it's unloaded and ready to depart is the oldest trick in the book. But I say we take it as soon as it docks."

"I still don't think it's going to work." I sighed.

"I have friends here; I told you that. Some of them served with me they know the charges against me are false." Kheda folded her arms over her chest.

"But you did disobey orders." I pointed out.

"Those are the charges the public heard. My prison paperwork and the part the public didn't see was that I was found guilty of treason." She explained.

"Treason? But why?" I sat up and struggled to keep my voice down.

"It's too much to tell you now. This is your last chance if you want out."

"No, it's been too late since the day I met you." She stared at me "So, what's your plan?"

The supply ship came once a week like clockwork. We were going to hit it hard and fast before the guards put two and two together. Her friends turned out to be some of the guards, and we're going to have us on unloading duty that day along with Dan. Artemis didn't really trust him, but she agreed that we needed the additional muscle at least until we got to the first trade ship. She got herself on unload duty the week before we planned to leave to be sure nothing had changed. She mapped out the timing and had it coordinated like a proper military operation.

We went to bed the night before our planned departure confident that one way or another it would be our last night there. I woke in the middle of the night feeling something was wrong. The door was still closed, but I knew something was off. I felt Kheda tense beside me, and I grabbed the scalpel she'd stolen from the hospital ward that I'd hidden beneath my pillow. In the faint glow of light from the window in the door, I saw someone approaching our bed. The person had a gun.

They aimed at Kheda, ready to kill her in her sleep. As quickly as I could I cut the tendons in the wrist holding the weapon. As the gun fell to the ground, Kheda swept his legs. He fell, bringing his throat into striking range. I cut his windpipe hoping to avoid too much blood. Kheda pushed him backward and picked up the gun. "A plasma rifle. How did he get this?"

"I want to know who it is." I went to the door and opened the window wider. It wasn't much, but I could see our attacker's face. It was Dan.

"Why would he do this? We were going to take him with us." Kheda narrowed her brows.

"I don't know, but they know we are planning to escape tomorrow. We have to still get out somehow."

"You're right. I'm just glad I didn't tell Dan everything."

"You didn't?" She asked surprised.

"No, I just told him to meet us at breakfast, and we'd fill him in."

"You brilliant man." Kheda hugged me.

"I never really trusted him either."

I went to check on the others, but Crow and Jim were dead. I guess Dan didn't want to risk us having any other allies. We pushed Dan under my bed and threw the blanket over him then climbed into his bed. We couldn't sleep after that. We both kept waiting for someone else to come after us. Finally, we agreed to sleep in shifts, and she was first. She laid her head in my lap, and her breath fell into a steady rhythm as I stroked her hair. I watched her as she slept one hand on her shoulder the other on the plasma rifle. She protested when I woke her a few hours later for her watch.

She woke me when she heard footsteps headed our direction. We both tensed as the door opened and the light came on. Salea stood in the doorway surveying the room. I thought we were caught for sure. "Get dressed; come on."

Kheda relaxed and began to get dressed. "Jack, hurry up."

I pulled on my boots since she still had my shirt. "What's Salea doing here?" I asked her quietly.

"One of my friends." She smiled.

"Major the ships due in early you must hurry." Salea urged watching for signs of anyone else.

"It's never early." She said pulling on her shirt. "Where are the others?"

"It's just Teesa and I," he said sadly. We'd been betrayed. Someone didn't want us getting out.

I got up and tucked in my shirt. "It's not just you Salea. Dan thought to murder us in our sleep." He nodded.

"I'll put them on lockdown let's go." Kheda was already moving past me with the plasma rifle in hand. Salea sealed the door as I came out and walked ahead. He took the gun from Kheda and put work chains on each of us but didn't bother locking them. He grinned at me before pushing us ahead.

"Just follow my lead and try not to get hurt," Kheda said quietly in English.

"What happened to the plan?" I was worried.

"Everything has changed." She shrugged.

I saw three other guards as we approached the cargo bay. All of them armed and placed strategically throughout the bay. Kheda noticed them too and was already appraising the situation. The guards seemed to relax once they saw us chained but still held their weapons at the ready. "It was just supposed to be one of them this morning." A fellow guard commented.

"Yeah well, the major insisted she come. She knocked out the humans when they tried to hold her back. I had to get a plasma rifle before she'd be quiet. She may not respect men, but she still respects a gun." Salea said annoyed as he pushed the barrel into her back for effect. The other guards laughed.

"I like to watch him work," Kheda growled and batted away the muzzle with a shoulder as she sat on a crate.

"You heard the major, Salea. Get him moving, and since he can't be trusted, he'll unload everything himself. Hope she hasn't been too rough on you, the ship is full this week." The guard mocked.

I rolled my eyes and held my hands out for Salea to unchain me. Salea reached for his key. "Leave them on." The other guard called.

"Have you seen those crates? I'll never pick them up if I can't get my arms around them." I protested. I knew they probably had lift equipment but was hoping for any excuse to get the chains off.

"Fine, do it your way then human." Salea took the chains off, and I headed into the cargo ship. The pilot was already heading out content to sit with the others and watch me work. He sat down by Kheda, and I knew he was the key to our escape. I came out a minute later with a medium crate and saw Kheda smack the pilot. The guards were on their feet, and Salea shoved the muzzle into her back again. In one fluid motion, she grabbed the gun and turned it on Salea. She shot him in the shoulder then dove behind a crate. The guards turned their guns on me. And I stooped behind my crate, but it would only protect me so long.

The lights went out, and the hazard lights came on. Someone tripped the emergency decompression signal. The doors slammed shut sealing one of the guards out of the room and keeping any others from coming to the rescue. In the confusion, Kheda shot another guard as he bared down on my position. I used the opportunity to run into the ship. The pilot followed me in. He swung high, and I ducked low. He caught me with a punch in my side and stunned me for a moment. I managed to sweep his legs as he stood gloating. I jumped on top of him before he got up again and punched him as hard as I could. I could have knocked him cold and left it at that, but suddenly this Kelsairan represented everyone that had tried to hurt Kheda. I hate to admit it, but then I snapped his neck. It was only fear for her that made me do it, but I did it just the same. Kheda came in rifle still in hand and stared at me as I climbed off the pilot.

"Is he dead?" she asked simply. I nodded. "Start the engines. I'll drag him off."

"Kheda let me..." I started not wanting her to handle the dead man.

"Jack go," I went to the cockpit and sat down to start the engines. Only moments later I heard the hatch close. Kheda sat down beside me and started checking the ship's systems. "I killed the two guards." She admitted quietly.

"And Salea?"

"Still cursing at me," she said with a hint of a smile. So it was settled we both did what we felt we had to do. Or at least that's what I let her think for quite some time.

Kheda used the codes Teesa gave her to open the bay doors, and we launched faster than we should have, but it was a good thing we did. Kras it seems is well armed, and they opened fire without warning. I managed to dodge the fire with little effort, so they launched two ships. I looked to Kheda worried. "Kelsairan ships are always armed."

"You fly. I'll shoot you don't need to kill any more of your own people today." She brought up weapons and took over flight controls. I managed to disable one of the ships as it left the launch bay but the second one proved much more difficult. Kheda's rolling and dodging to avoid the shots from Kras didn't help much either. Finally, she looped back, and I caught the other ship with a lucky shot to their engines. The ship exploded almost instantly.

"Good shot. They only had two ships we should be safe for the moment I'd better get to work." She said as she got up and headed for the cargo hold.

Chapter 7

Once we were safely away from Kras, I put us on autopilot. I went to the back to see how Kheda was doing on altering our engines and beacon signal. She was covered in dirt and up to her elbows in circuitry. "How's it going?"

"It's easier to do when the beacons not being used." She complained. "The engines are done at least. You should double back a little way to confuse them then head off course."

"I already did." I liked watching her work.

"I'm beginning to think escaping was the easy part." She said as she bunched circuits together and pushed them back into the panel. She stood and wiped her brow.

"I knew it would be. Just take it one step at a time." I looked around at the full cargo hold of the ship. "At least we have enough to barter for a new ship."

"Stealing from my own people." She said disgustedly. I found her a bottle of water and handed it to her. She took a long drink.

I pulled her close and kissed her. "At least you don't have to hit me all the time."

"Maybe I like hitting you," Kheda said. I shook my head, and she looked away a moment. "Then at least the beard can go now?"

"Part of it." I agreed. "There's one shower. Why don't you use it first."

Kheda wiggled out of my arms with a smile. "So you can get me dirty again when I'm done? No, you go ahead." She said as she headed up to the controls.

I went to the small bedroom if you could call it that. The bed pulled out of the wall, and the bathroom just had a curtain hung over the door. I took off my dirty prison issue pants and shirt and stepped into the shower. The first private shower I'd had in seven months. I turned on the water; it was lukewarm but better than the cold water on Kras. I found a small hand mirror and used the knife Salea gave me to shave. I only left the beard around my mouth and chin. I knew Kheda wanted it all gone, but we had to be practical. I didn't want to be recognized after the trade ship. If I left part of the beard, then I could shave the rest later.

I came out of the bedroom freshly dressed in the clothes Salea hid on board. They were Kelsairan and a little tight in the chest. The shirt was long and tan with long sleeves. The neckline was round with a deep v in front, and the trim matched the cuffs. There were black pants that matched and were just barely big enough.

Kheda smiled at me. "You still don't look Kelsairan. But you are handsome." It was the first compliment she gave me. "and I still don't like the beard. She stood before me looking me in the eye. It still seemed odd for a woman to match my height of 6'2." She moved to kiss me, and I stepped away.

"What was that about getting you dirty?"

"I'm already dirty," Kheda said innocently.

"But I'm not."I pointed out. She smiled again and headed to the back.

She came back a short while later dressed in a similar fashion only in a pink top. Her hair was still wet but not slicked back like usual. "You look beautiful, whether you're dirty or clean," I told her when she sat down beside me. "But I miss your perfume."

"Jack," she started then thought a moment. "If your name is Jackson, where did Jeep come from?"

I laughed a moment thinking about it. "In boot camp, they give you old-fashioned tags until you're done with basic training then you get your implant. The tags have your personal information including your full name. One of the guys saw mine and realized my initials were close JEP. The name just stuck, I guess."

"What's your full name then?"

"Jackson Eli Peterson. No one calls me Jack, by the way. I was worried they'd figure out I was military if I used Jackson.What about you? How'd you pick Artemis?"

"My father loved your people's stories. He read them to me when I was little. I wanted something that was feminine but could be shortened. So, I picked Artemis; she was my favorite, anyway. And Trekes; well, Trekes was the name of one of our great scholars a real whiz at mathematics."

"Wait, Trekes isn't your last name either?" She shook her head. "What is it then?"

"Ailaryia, A-lair-ye-a," she said it slowly for me. "All to protect our families." She sighed.

"Why did they accuse you of treason?" I looked over at her.

She shook her head. "Not yet; I still don't know if it's safe." She looked around the ship. I wasn't sure if she was just being paranoid or if she had a good reason, but I didn't press her. "I wanted to be an engineer when I joined the army did I tell you?" I shook my head.

"My father was a professor at the university. I guess it runs in my blood. I was assigned as ships engineer to a small ten man ship on a long haul from Kelsair to a storage depot. We were attacked, and the pilot was killed. The commanding officer was unconscious, and suddenly I was the only one left who could fly, or at least the only one who would admit I could.

The others wanted to surrender, hoping the humans would leave us to drift if we didn't resist. I took the controls and assigned a gunner. I lost two more men, but we knocked out three human crafts and got safely to the surface. That's as much fighting as I ever wanted to see but once the officers on Kelsair heard the news, I was placed in officer training myself and special ops. I got a medal out of it. I still wish I'd stayed an engineer and never grabbed those controls."

"Then you and I would have never met." I took her hand.

"And I wouldn't have ruined your life." She frowned.

"I'd hardly say ruined I'd still be in Kras now if not for you." She cheered up a little. "What happened to your father?" She looked at me confused "You said he was a professor."

"My mother persuaded him to get into politics, and he's a diplomat now. It pays far better, but he's not as happy."

"It's been a long day; maybe you should get some sleep." I was worried about her.

"I'm not tired, you go ahead."

I pulled the bed out and lay down hating the fact that we had to sleep on opposite schedules for a while. I'd gotten so used to Kheda sleeping beside me that I wondered now if I could sleep. I twisted and turned unable to get comfortable in the constricting clothes so I took them off hoping Kheda would stay at the controls. I fell into a fitful sleep that soon turned to dreams of her. I woke up hours later relieved that we were sleeping apart but feeling guilty about the dreams I'd had. Then she was in the doorway.

"I was just coming to wake you. Did you sleep well?"

"No, I'm worried."

"Not too worried, I see," she nodded at me. I pulled the blankets around me like an embarrassed thirteen-year-old. She merely smiled and left so I could get dressed.

I came out a few minutes later, and she was at the controls. "Kheda, I..." I started but had no idea what to say.

"Jackson, how many years have I been around men? It happens to all of us, it just not as embarrassing for women. Now, can I get some sleep?" I nodded dumbfounded.

Chapter 8

It took three days to get to the trade ship. Any time both of us were awake, one of us would inventory the cargo hold to see precisely what we had to bargain with. The ship could fly itself, but we didn't want to chance anyone sneaking up on us. For being in such close quarters, we actually spent very little time together. We docked at the trade ship with only having passed one ship, and it was a small merchant vessel that had no need to notice us much less hail us.

Kheda went off in search of supplies for the next leg of our journey dressed in her Kelsairan clothes and some kind of hat and veil. I went to look up an old friend that was supposed to have a restaurant here. I hoped he could tell me who would be interested in the ship so I wouldn't have to advertise. Tony's was in the corner of the food market and crammed with humans and aliens. I pushed my way through to the bar and found Tony behind it. "What can I get you, sir?" he asked without looking up.

"How about an ice cold Bud." I knew he couldn't get it out here, but I also knew it would get his attention. I told him he owed me one the last time I saw him.

He looked up. "Jackson, what the hell are you doing here?" he looked around "Where's Jeannie?"

"Is there somewhere we can talk?" I looked around the bar.

He nodded "Lirs," he waved over a blue-skinned telaithan female. She took over for him, and we headed for the back.

"Looks like you're doing well."

"It started as an Italian place, but then I added Chinese and then Thai. They can't get enough of our food. And for you, I could find a Bud." He grinned.

"I just wanted to get your attention." He pushed open an office door, and I went in. He sat down at his desk, and I sat across from him.

"So what brings you here of all places. It looks like your out of the army." He said noticing my long hair and beard.

I looked around the room. "Is it safe to talk in here?"

"Of course, Jackson; why are you so paranoid?" He leaned back in his chair and put his feet up.

"Because I'm still in the army or, at least, I should be," I confessed.

"You went AWOL?" His feet clunked to the floor as he jerked straight in his chair.

"No, MIA. I was captured and taken to Kras. I've been there for seven months." I fidgeted not comfortable with everything that happened. "And they let you out?" He asked. I stared at him. "You actually escaped from Kras?"

"I had help. My partner's getting supplies." I looked around the room nervous.

"And you trust him not to leave you behind?" Tony scratched his head.

"I have to; she's all I have right now," I said quietly.

"She? Oh, Jackson, what have you gotten yourself into now? Please tell me she's at least human." Tony, pleaded. I shook my head. "What then, Kelsairan?" he started to laugh then stopped when I didn't.

"I need three things from you, and one is for your safety more than anything else."

"All right, Jackson." Tony sighed.

"Say nothing to anyone about seeing me and get this to my parents they'll be worried." I handed him a letter I'd written during one of my many stints at the controls.

"Done and the third?"

"I have a ship with a full cargo hold to get rid of and fast."

"I know the guy to do it, but he won't like that you stole it. He pretends to have morals, even though he's as dishonest as the rest of them." Tony scrounged on his desk for the man's name.

"We already have a story schemed up."

Tony found the name and his communicator "What is it? I have to call him, or he won't see you." I told Tony the story, and he couldn't stop shaking his head. "It's believable except for you married to a Kelsairan." He hailed his contact.

"Tony, friend; you not call me long time how I help you?" It was a Zalean on the other end. They all had the same speech pattern.

"I have a friend that just came to see me, Dex; he has an interesting proposition for you. You could stand to make a nice profit."

"This friend bring good fortune." Definitely a Zalean. They lived their life by chance and luck.

"He and his wife are selling a cargo ship with a loaded hold. Are you interested?"

"Why they not sell pieces themselves? Why sell to Dex to do?"

"They aren't merchants they took this ship in trade for their own hoping to earn a little extra money, looks like my friend is about to be a dad."

"Excellent fortune; send them." The transmission ended. Tony looked at me.

"Great, she's going to kill me."

"It was your story." He chided me before giving me directions to Dex's office.

I nodded. "Thanks, Tony. I'll send word when I can, but it looks like I'll be on the run for a while."

"I understand," He gave me a big hug and pat me on the back. I turned to leave, but he stopped me "Jackson, is she at least pretty?"

"She's gorgeous," I grinned at him, and he shooed me out the door.

Luckily Kheda was already back at the ship. She was meditating on the bed with the few bags she bought next to her. I rested against the doorframe, and she opened her eyes. "I have good news and bad news. I found a buyer, but he wants us both to come."

"Somehow I thought you would say that I was praying now for patience and that we could pull this off. I also bought big enough garments in the market." I smiled at her. She thought of everything I did not. These were the exact reasons I fell in love with her and was getting myself in deeper every day. Although at this point I hadn't admitted it to myself. I knew I cared a great deal about her, but I wasn't yet willing to admit I loved one of the enemies.

"All right, get changed, and we'll go." I took one last stroll through the cargo hold making sure everything was in order and picked up the inventory. She came out a few minutes later dressed in a blue dress. She'd padded her breasts and had a convincing belly.

She looked to me "Is it convincing?"

"I'd say so." She came closer and put my hands on her fake belly. It was hard and somewhat cool to the touch. "What is that?"

"Some kind of fruit. I was worried, sometimes people want to touch it." I nearly laughed at her ingenuity. She grabbed the hat and veils she was wearing earlier, and we left the ship. I followed Tony's directions and found Dex's office quickly. The lights were off though, and I was worried. I knocked on the door anyway.

"Who there?" came a meek voice.

"Not a Zalean." Kheda cursed.

"Tony's friend."

The door swung open, and a light came on "Come in good fortune." The office was no more than a metal box with stacks of boxes everywhere with a desk in the center.

"Oh, and beautiful wife," he started then noticed she was Kelsairan. "I see war for you two not exist. Beware those who dislike half-breeds." He ushered us in and offered Kheda the only chair.

"What type ship, friend?"

"A Kelsairan cargo ship with a 65 square meter hold. We took an inventory." I handed over the pad. Dex eyed over the list.

"Yes, see not much of real value. Some weapons and food, oh medical supplies. Well, maybe. What you want friend?"

"We need another ship to get home and some money for our baby."

Dex scratched his chin. "What kind ship?"

"Something to get us to the Navea system before our child is born," I told him.

"When?" He scanned the inventory again.

"Two, three weeks tops." I looked to Kheda who rubbed her fake belly.

"You cut close," Dex complained. "I have small telaithan cruiser big bed for wife." I looked to Kheda who was not only a whiz with ships but knew what could get into Kelsairan space. She nodded. Dex went to his desk and found his handheld inventory and pulled up the list. He ran some kind of search and handed me the list. "You pick one item here to sell when you get home worth good money all."

"I said money, Dex. I'm no merchant."

"Dex has no money all in trade." I took the list and handed it to Kheda hoping she could figure out what to trade. Dex looked at me.

"She has a head for business. I'm just the pilot." Kheda looked up at me and smiled then looked back to the list. Dex tried to see what she was looking at but had no luck.

Kheda got to the end of the list "Ah, here we go the Ceron ale."

"But," Dex started.

"It was on your list." Kheda countered.

Dex looked to me "This contingent on everything in cargo hold as listed on your inventory."

"Agreed, right down to the last bandage." I offered him my hand, and he accepted. "We just need to get our personal things and meet you at dock 12 in a half hour." Dex nodded.

"You mind?" he asked Kheda. She nodded, and he rubbed her fake belly. "Two? Good fortune." He looked to me. I merely smiled in reply.

The trade went off without a hitch, and the new ship was smaller. It had better living quarters though. The bedroom could actually be called that, and the bathroom was larger with a sink shower and toilet. There was a little kitchen with a food replicator. It was broken, but Kheda said she could fix it. The case of ceron ale sat on the table waiting for us like a prize the bottles were dusty, but Kheda said that was a good thing. I let her settle in while I went to prepare to leave.

Once we were on a heading to kelsair, I found her again meditating on the bed. Something seemed to be bothering her today. She'd changed into the pink Kelsairan shirt, and black pants and her body was back to normal. She opened her eyes finally "Are we headed to Kelsair?"

"We are, and no one is following."

"Good; you rest since you've been up the longest." She said calmly.

"Kheda, is there something you wanted to tell me?"

"Not right now; you rest." She got up and left.

I put on the new pants she bought me. Then lay in bed thinking I was crazy for letting her take me to Kelsair, of all places. I assured myself everything would be fine. I still didn't know why we were going there, but she promised to tell me. Maybe that's what was bothering her. I fell asleep finally and dreamed they were taking us back to Kras. I woke up in a cold sweat hours later. I got out of bed and rushed to find Kheda. She stared at me when I ran into the little kitchen like a boy longing for his mother. But I was so relieved to see her I didn't really care. What they were doing to her in my dream was far worse than what they were doing to me.

Kheda went to the replicator and made me a cup of coffee without my asking. I sat down at the table, and she brought it over. I savored the taste my first cup of coffee in eight months, and it was exactly what

I needed. She glanced at the monitor as she sat down. She'd rerouted some of the controls here while she worked.

"Jackson, there are things I must tell you, and I fear what you will say to me. I only ask that you listen to me openly and believe me when I say I never meant to hurt you."

I looked at her she hadn't hurt me at least not yet. I took a big swig of coffee bracing myself for what she would say. "Go on."

"Our meeting was not an accident." I nearly choked on my coffee. "The Kelsairan army had been scanning planets in the neutral territories for soldiers alone on planets. My ship was packed and ready for months as I waited for someone to land and was never far from me should the opportunity arise."

"Special Ops," I commented, and she nodded "So I was a mission."

"Not you specifically. The target had to be male and an officer. You just happened to be the first to fit the criteria. I'm sorry."

"So what was your mission?"

"To gain your trust, then you were to be found and captured. I was to be sent to prison, and we would escape."

"Sounds like you're on task to me." I was getting angrier by the minute.

"I'm not, Jackson. I was supposed to feed you information on a false attack on the Sirus system and show you our troop movements all in hopes of luring the human army into a major ambush."

"Who's to say you won't?" I got up from the table and went to the bedroom. I shut the door. I couldn't look at her. I could hear her come after me and talk through the door.

"If I was going to would I tell you now?" I sighed. Kheda had a point. She begged and pleaded with me to come out and, finally, I caved. Maybe I shouldn't have. Perhaps, I should have told her to drop me at the next trade ship with a bottle of ale so I could barter my way home but I didn't. I opened the door.

"So, tell me everything from the beginning. Maybe then I can trust you again." I went back to the kitchen, and she followed, looking utterly lost and defeated. I'd never seen her like that before; not when she was injured and not at her trial. That was nearly enough to convince me there, but I was hurt beyond comprehension that she would keep it from me for so long. She sat down across from me.

"I got the call that you were headed for Micea. My transport dropped me off, ship and all. I rigged one engine months ago to go out. The second wasn't supposed to follow. I wanted to crash, but I also wanted to live through it. I used a loose piece of metal to cut my leg open. Just as I started, it is when the engine cut out that's why it was so deep. I barely got it tied off enough to keep from bleeding out before I had to return to the controls. God, I thought I was going to die. I managed to keep her level, but I was knocked unconscious. That wasn't supposed to happen either. I knew I was dead when everything went black.

"Then I woke and you were there. I was safe. You weren't what I was expecting. You weren't supposed to be handsome, or kind, or charming. I half expected to be raped, and somehow I justified it as part of my duty. I even used my body to my advantage. I figured if you had what you wanted from me it would be easier to gain your trust. You didn't, though, and it intrigued me.

"I had this whole scheme in mind, but nothing seemed to go right. My ship was wrecked so I had nothing and I couldn't get a bio signature for my trial. The only thing that worked in my favor was the osimpas, but even they proved more trouble than I thought. I was going to offer not shooting you as a simple repayment and leave it at that, but you Jackson, had to make me care for you. Twelve years around men in the military and I never met anyone like you. Everything I said and did I meant. You met the real me not Major Trekes, the persona I put on when I go to war."

"Thank you, for that much at least," I said, still hurt. Khenda reached for my hand, and I pulled away.

"God Jackson, do you know how hard it was for me to resist you? How hard it still is?" She sighed and looked away.

"Go on with your story," I told her, not wanting to hear it.

"I thought about you every night for weeks, and my men were beginning to think something happened between us. So, I pushed you out of my head. Still, occasionally, I would dream of you. Months drifted by without any word or sign of you and I thought you were gone. Every fight I was in, I would scan for your beacon and civilians before attacking. My men had the same orders."

I looked at her surprised. "I killed four of your men."

"They were told you were a good pilot, evasive maneuvers until I got to you. They shot back but not to kill. You forget I killed five of yours." I nodded point taken "My debt was not so easily paid Jackson you saved me more than once on Micea. My men understood and gladly honored that debt. The transport ship outside Navea was not the only one your words spared either. Three others were only disabled."

"Why was Navea the one you were on trial for then?"

"They were looking for you still hoping to go through with their plan. The army couldn't find you though and finally grew sick of my disruption. Other units were beginning to scan for civilians as well, and the government didn't like their authority being questioned. I was hauled before the tribunal, and I thought I would go ahead with my mission as planned. But the trial didn't go the way it should. They began asking about the other ships and my orders to my men. They asked nothing of you.

"When I had to bring you up in my own defense I realized my mission no longer existed. The task I risked my life and my virtue on, was all for nothing. I'd never felt so betrayed in my life. Then they brought out accusations that you and I had been intimate and I was outraged. They forged tapes of you and I using pieces of real footage spliced with footage taken later at the base. It wasn't even the same room, but people believed what they wanted to think.

"So I told them exactly what I thought of their precious war and everything I'd told my men about humans. Officially I was found guilty of failure to obey orders and sent to Roteo but off the records. I was found guilty of treason and sent to Kras. I thought for sure I'd die there and didn't really care. I was at peace with my god, and that was enough. Then when those men attacked instinct took over."

"I noticed, I'm glad we met as friends before enemies."

"Then, you were there. I thought somehow my mission was never canceled. That perhaps the army merely had to trump up the charges to get me into Kras to get to you. But then you told me about the official, and I knew I was wrong. They didn't know you were there. They thought somehow I would have been stupid enough to give you my name or that you had somehow figured it out. Looking back, I suppose I should have given them someway to locate you. Looking back I don't think I wanted them to find you. If they did it would mean I would have to hurt you and put you in danger and I couldn't do it.

"I started off with five friends in the jail, all of them guards well except Teesa. One was a childhood friend and the rest I served within the army. Salea and I were together on that small ten man ship I told you about he was my gunner. Teesa is his wife. They went undercover; in case you got sent there, he was to figure out who you were and was my contact on Kras."

"Why didn't they pull him out?" I turned my coffee cup in my hands.

"Because the government underestimates the power of loyalty of Kelsairan to Kelsairan. They believe there can only be loyalty to the government. They thought Salea would keep me there simply because he was in the army."

"That's why you shot him to make it look like he was doing his duty."

She nodded glumly. "That and Teesa is carrying their child. He'll never hold a gun right again; they'll give him a nice desk job now, and Teesa won't have to worry."

I shook my head in disbelief before asking, "Why are we going to Kelsair?"

"For help. My brother has a ship that won't be recognized, and he can give us money. I also have to get my journal and the fake plans my government wanted to feed yours I was hoping they could do something with them."

"How do I know this isn't some trap?"

"Jackson, why would I tell you all this if it was?"

"Why didn't you tell me sooner if it wasn't?"

"Jackson, I wanted to but I couldn't. I was afraid the prison, and even the transport ship was bugged. I'm talking about trying to end the war and maybe even doing so by letting the humans win. I really am committing treason. I have every right to be paranoid and secretive."

"And why, all of a sudden, are you so concerned with ending the war?"

"Because only when the war is over can we truly be together." She looked away from me ready to cry. "God, Jackson, I love you. I didn't mean for it to happen but I do. I don't care what happens; I just want to be with you." I knew then I loved her too because at that moment I forgave every lie she told me and secret she kept. "You don't have to say the same just forgive me." She pleaded.

"Kheda, I forgive you. Although, it will take me a while to trust you again." I told her. She came around the table and fell into my arms. She cried there softly a few moments until my arms finally wrapped around her. "Why don't you rest for a while."

"You swear you'll be here when I wake up?" Kheda looked up at me.

"Kheda, where would I go? Besides, I can't stop without risking your life, and no matter how mad I am I can't do that." She wiped her tears and smiled hearing the implications in my voice. "Now you're happy? Women," I said exasperated "go get some sleep." She got up and went into the bedroom while I went for more coffee.

Chapter 9

Kheda spent the next three days figuring out how to fool the sensors into showing two Kelsairan biosignatures. The best she managed so far was a Kelsairan and Ceron. It wasn't perfect, but it wasn't what they were looking for either. I watched her as she worked. I know I should have remained angry with her longer and should have kept my distance, but I couldn't. There was something about her that I found utterly irresistible. Whether it was her calm confidence, her intelligence, or just her good looks; I don't know, but I found it hard to keep my distance. I still had not told her I loved her though, but I had admitted it to myself. That, to me, seemed to be punishment enough for her.

I got nervous when we entered Kelsairan space. The ships ignored us for the most part. Two days of travel brought us to Kelsair. Our view screen worked, although it would not transmit a picture somehow, Kheda simply couldn't fix it. Kelsair seemed a small planet, but there appeared to be more water than on earth. There were lush bands of green and stretches of brown. "I grew up there on that land mass below that band of forest. We are headed here to this forest one of my parent's homes is there."

I glanced at the control panel. "Kheda were being hailed."

"Try not to speak you still have an accent." She grinned at me. "This is Sai; we humbly request permission to land."

"What's your business on Kelsair?" The voice was flat on the other end of the comm.

"I've come to pay homage to Kelta," Kheda said respectfully.

"And the Ceron?" The voice was annoyed now.

"My husband." She took my hand. We both wanted more than what we had now.

"You have three days." The voice was flat again.

"I would like to visit family," Kheda told the voice.

"Four and do so quickly. Next time be sure your view screen is transmitting." The voice nearly growled at us.

"Sorry, I can't seem to figure out what the problem is." She held up a severed wire and grinned. She cut off the transmission and looked at me. "I was hoping for five days. We'll just have to hope my brother is near. We'll set the ship on autopilot to take off in four days if we get the ship from my brother. We won't have to worry about anyone finding it."

"And if we can't?" I looked at her worried.

"We'll have to hurry back. Tonight, though, you'll have a real Kelsairan meal." She was getting excited.

"Are you cooking?" I was skeptical. Kheda didn't seem like the domesticated type.

She shook her head, "No, my aunt will."

"I don't think it's a good idea to see your family."

"Aunt Sai wouldn't care if you were an osimpa. If I love you, then she'll love you."

"That's how you thought of that name so quickly." I grabbed her and stole a kiss it was the first since she confessed. She kissed me back and lingered in my arms. "What was that about someone loving me?"

"I do, but you won't hear me repeat it until you say the same." She pulled away as if she were mad at me and sat down at the controls.

"Kheda, who's Kelta?"

"Our god."

I looked at her surprised. "I never heard you call him by name before."

"We do not speak his name in front of outsiders." She looked down then at me.

"But I am an outsider."

Kheda took my hand, "Not to me, Jackson. Over the past few months, you've shown more devotion to me than any of my own people."

"Kheda..." I was going to tell her I loved her then, but the mood was all wrong. I just couldn't bring myself to do it. "thank you." I said stupidly then cursed myself.

We landed at the edge of a lush forest beside a small house. There was a vegetable garden growing out front and some kind of vineyard on the hills north of the home. An older woman came outside. She was as tall as Kheda with the same blonde hair and blue eyes. But her hair was longer and fell in a braid down her back. She wore a white dress that blew in the breeze. A man came out and stood beside her. He was big, even for a Kelsairan, and was nearly seven foot tall. His hair and eyes were both dark, and he looked like he'd just been discharged from the military. I stared at Kheda worried.

"That's just uncle Tam. He won't hurt you but let me go first to warn them." She moved ahead of me.

"You have to warn them?"

"How would your family respond?" I nodded then understanding. She ran out to greet them, and her uncle scooped her up like she was still a little girl. Her aunt hugged her as well happy to see her. They looked at her then peered around to the ship. Kheda waved me out. I took a deep breath and went to meet them.

"He's big for a human, Kheda," I heard her uncle say.

"I thought the same of you when I saw you," I said in Kelsairan and surprised him. "I hope we can be friends."

Her uncle smiled "This one's funny,"

"I'm Jackson," I said introducing myself.

"I'm Tam, my wife Sai."

"Well, come on in dinner isn't going to cook itself." Aunt Sai ushered us in.

Uncle Tam grabbed my arm "I'm going to show him the vines." He called to his wife.

"You behave," she called back.

Tam took me to the hills, and I was surprised to see grapes growing. "Where did you get these?"

"The original plants were brought before the war began. I'm one of the only Kelsairans that can make wine. Granted, our tastes are a little different from yours, but the Kelsairans like it just the same. I get quite a premium." He sat down in the dirt and waited for me to do the same. "What kind of trouble are you two in?"

"You don't want to know I think it's better you not get involved."

"What did you have to do to escape Kras?"

"Kheda didn't think you would know."

"Sai doesn't, but I have a monitor in my workshop. I saw her trial, and I'm assuming your Jeep."

"Sir, nothing happened between her and me."

"I know," he pulled off a grape inspected it then popped it in his mouth. "I know my niece better than that. Besides, that recording was horrible. So how much trouble are you in?"

"A lot, Kheda stands convicted of treason." Tam nearly choked on another grape. "The army was killing human civilians, and she wanted to put a stop to it."

Tam nodded. "That's my niece. What are you going to do now?"

"Find her brother for a ship and money then retrieve some papers she thinks can help end the war."

"Do you really think so?" He tilted his head.

"No, but what choice do we have?" I didn't think she had a chance in hell of ending the war. We didn't have any other options though so we had to try.

"Ah, I see now. You know there are others that have made it work despite the war." He sat back.

"Others, but not *the* Major Trekes,"

"She is just Kheda now." Her uncle pointed out as he got up. "Come on let's go see where Aya is."

Her uncle found out where Kheda's brother was by searching the entertainment news and we headed back to the house. It was just in time too Kheda, and her aunt were setting the food on the table. "Can you eat Kelsairan food?" her aunt asked.

"I'm willing to try it; it looks wonderful," I told her. Aunt Sai looked to Kheda and smiled.

"You two go wash up. I know you've been playing in the dirt." Aunt Sai scolded us as we tried to sit down.

Her uncle showed me where I could wash up, and I asked if he had a razor, of course not, Kelsairans didn't need to shave. He did give me an extremely sharp knife that made quick work of my beard. I came back out, and both women smiled in approval. I tried a little bit of everything and had no idea what I was eating although I liked it all. Kheda watched me close wondering how I would react to particular dishes. I'm confident she thought I'd hate it. Her aunt seemed pleased though, and her uncle was jolly company. We laughed throughout dinner and well past dessert.

After I helped Kheda clear the table and wash the dishes, we went for a walk just as we had on Micea. The stars were different, and the lake was absent, but it was no less romantic. She'd found more of her perfume somewhere, and it drifted on the breeze. I didn't want to break the spell, but I couldn't hide my appreciation. "I see you found more of your perfume."

"I borrowed some of Aunt Sai's it's the same scent. I know how much you like it." She looked at me "I see your beard is finally gone."

"I know how much you hated it." I smiled at her.

She took both my hands in hers and laid her head on my chest. "Do you trust me again Jackson?"

"I never truly stopped. You just hurt me Kheda that you kept such a secret from me." Took a deep breath and let it out.

"I thought I would lose you forever." She snuggled in closer.

"You won't, Kheda; I love you," I confessed.

"Do you, Jackson?" Kheda looked up at me.

"I have for a long time. I just couldn't admit it." I kissed her, and she melted into my arms.

"Jackson, be with me tonight please?" I was surprised it's not exactly what I was expecting. She was finally ready to be with me, and I was having doubts.

I looked at her, and she was serious. "First, tell me why you wouldn't on Micea."

"We were enemies."

"No, the second night when you said: 'I can't.'"

She turned away from me. "Did I say that?"

"Kheda, you know you did. Something changed in your thinking that night. It was no longer about us being enemies; it was an internal struggle so tell me why."

She looked at me "Jackson, I've never been with a man." I was stunned after everything I heard it wasn't what I was expecting.

"But the rumors..." I stammered like an idiot.

"Are just that. I let my men claim what they wanted because it helped their reputation and did nothing to mine. In the army, it's acceptable for women to do so."

"But you didn't?" I was confused now.

"It was a personal choice Kelta asks that we remain pure until we marry as an act of discipline and self-control." She looked up at the stars.

I wrapped my arms around her from behind "So why give up now?"

"Jackson does it look like I'm going to marry, I mean you and I..." now she was the one stammering like an idiot.

"Kheda, I would like nothing more than for you to be my wife." I kissed the top of her head.

"Jackson, be reasonable. How would it ever work? We'd both be exiles."

"Like we're not already? Besides, you're the one with a scheme to end the war, remember?"

"And if I can't?" Kheda's shoulders sagged.

"Who cares, I love you. Lately, it seems everything in my life has been about you anyway so why not make it official?"

She turned in my arms to face me. "This is the craziest thing you've ever thought of."

"It certainly beats our last relationship." I smiled at her. She laughed.

"I love you, Jackson."

"Is that a yes?" I squeezed her tighter.

"I must be as crazy as you are, yes." She kissed me again, and I'd never been happier or more worried. "Can we go to bed now?"

"Only to sleep, you've waited this long a little longer won't kill you." She looked genuinely disappointed but happy at the same time. I think it surprised her that I would be so understanding. I'd waited a long time to be with her too, a. A little longer wasn't going to kill me either, although resisting her was going to be the hard part. Just the thought of having her near for the rest of my life was a turn on like I never thought it would be. Then there was the fact that we were still on the run I felt like I was in high school again sneaking around with Mindy Jenkins.

She slept in my arms that night content to be near me. I wondered what her aunt and uncle would say in the morning. She said I shouldn't worry. She was going to tell them about our engagement. The thought scared me. How much more danger could we place these two in? She assured me though everything would be fine and drifted off to sleep. I lay there watching her dream for a long time worried about our future. Finally, I fell asleep and before I knew it her aunt was on the door waking us for breakfast.

Kheda got up as if nothing were wrong and her aunt said nothing. Apparently, I had less reason to worry than I thought. Kheda opened a drawer and pulled out a one-piece outfit and laid it on the bed. "Do you keep clothes everywhere?"

"You never know what's going to happen." She smiled as she shut the door. She pulled off my t-shirt and threw it at me. I grabbed her and pulled her to the bed. "Let go, Jackson. What happened to our discussion last night?"

"You aren't playing fair." I protested.

"Let go; I have to dress." I snatched a kiss and let her go. Then I got out of bed and began to change into clean boxers. "What are you doing?"

"I have to get dressed."

She watched me as I pulled off my shorts. "But you never changed in front of me before."

"Suddenly you're shy?" I asked. She seemed at a loss for words. "Last night you wanted to be with me, and today I'm not allowed to change in front of you? We are still getting married, right?"

"Of course we are; I was just surprised," Kheda explained. I shook my head and pulled on my boxers. "Wait, I didn't get to see anything."

"Kheda, you're aunt is waiting."

"I've never seen a man before, and my future husband denies me?" she pouted. I gave in and dropped my shorts. She smiled at me, and I knew then I was already spoiling her. She stepped towards me and ran her hand down my chest. "I didn't realize your muscles would go all the way down." She said tracing the muscle that ran over my hip bone. She kissed me a long moment and glanced down then smiled. She moved away and got dressed. I pulled on my boxers and bundled up my clothes as I headed out the door. "Where are you going?"

"To take a cold shower," I called back, wondering how many cold showers I would have to endure before I married her. We were going to have a very long talk when we were alone.

I came downstairs and found everyone at breakfast. They were halfway done eating, but I really didn't care. I was never one who liked eating breakfast. I sat down beside Tam, and he smacked me on the back. "I told you that you could make it work. I'm glad you took my advice."

"I'll have a talk with my niece before you leave. Tam told me how unpleasant cold showers are." Sai smiled at me then looked to Kheda who actually blushed. I couldn't help but laugh I didn't think anyone could make her blush.

"Then we have your approval?" I asked them.

"Of course; anything Kheda wants it's always been that way. She had to renounce her parents and brother, but not her aunt and uncle were all the family she's had for years. But what she did for Aya; well, we can't help but be proud of her for that. And, if she is able to end this insanity, then so be it." Tam said, proudly looking to his niece. "Although, I'll have to persuade your father to pass a bill to stop the import of grapes."

"Tam really, Sen has more important things to do."

"I've never asked anything of my brother. If it weren't for Cime, he'd still be happy at the university."

"Uncle Tam, please." Kheda looked to him.

"You're right Kheda, sorry. Let's finish breakfast so you can go."

After breakfast, Kheda and her aunt had a chat just as she promised. Tam and I loaded a ground cruiser full of supplies and our personal belongings. "Watch out for Aya he's a little protective of his sister."

"Aya? Shouldn't it be the other way around?"

"Those two are very close. That's why she's going to him for help. But he won't be as understanding as we are. Let Kheda do the talking with him and, for Kelta's sake, don't get into a fight with him. He may be a singer, but he's still Kelsairan, and he has a lot of political pull."

"Point taken."

"Now I'll give you two weeks to get safely off the planet, but then I must call my brother. I always do when Kheda visits. I will tell him about your engagement."

"How do you think he'll take it?"

"I don't know. On the one hand, none of us thought Kheda would marry. Well, she couldn't and on the other hand. You're human. So, I simply don't know."

"Thanks, Tam."

"You're welcome Jackson; just take care of her." I looked at him. "You humans worry too much." He said as Kheda came up behind him.

"About what now? He's always worried about something." She grinned at me.

"And look where it's gotten me. Maybe I should stop worrying." I said sarcastically as I started the engine. Kheda climbed in beside me. "Where to?"

"Follow the road until we're out of the vineyard. We'll stay in our country home tonight and the lake house tomorrow."

"Can't we make it to Vali today?"

"Yes, but Aya won't be there until tomorrow. I might be recognized if we're there too long. We'll leave from the lake house that's where I left my journals and the documents for my mission."

"All right," I waved goodbye to her family and moved the cruiser out. For as clunky as the ship looked it was fast. Kheda merely smiled when I mentioned it.

The country home looked like something out of a fairy tale. It was nestled in the woods with daub walls and a thatch roof. There was an overgrown garden of wildflowers growing in front with bright orange and red flowers. Kheda punched in a code on the lock, and the door swung open. The furniture inside was covered in sheets, and the place smelled musty. She went to the control panel and turned on the lights and ventilation.

"There's a replicator in the kitchen. If you want to pick something for dinner, then I can make sure the bedroom and bathroom are in order."

"I think I can do that, but we might have the same dishes tonight as last night," I warned her. She smiled and headed upstairs with our bags. I watched her go in one of her skin-tight black one-piece outfits. I cleared my head, thinking if I didn't I would need another cold shower. I found the plates and silverware and set them on the counter. I also found two glasses for one of the bottles of wine Tam sent. I replicated the only two dishes I could remember the names for and set them down just as Kheda returned.

"Good choices," she commented as she pulled a stool out at the counter. I poured her a glass of wine without asking "I don't drink."

"Another discipline thing?"

"No, I just never liked it much."

"Just one glass with dinner. Your uncle sent this for us." She relented and finally and took a drink. "Not bad," she commented.

I sampled it as well. The wine was heavier and had more body; it was as if I could taste the foreign soil in the wine. "Quite nice, actually. Your uncle knows what he's doing; the people back home would love it."

"And this started as a human drink?"

"Thousands of years ago," I assured her. She nodded and scooped out what I thought were noodles on her plate.

"Do you know what this is, Jackson?"

"Don't tell me, Kheda; I like it, so let's just leave it at that." She laughed but agreed.

She had quite a few glasses of wine that night and ended up drunk. No one told me Kelsairans metabolized alcohol poorly. I carried her to bed and helped her undress. I moved to pull my t-shirt over her head, but she didn't want to put it on. She pulled me close instead and snuggled into my arms. She lay there a long time in my arms with her skin against mine.

It was then that I began to notice the scars she carried. Small cuts from fist and knife fights mostly. But on her left shoulder, she had a scar from being shot. I kissed it, but she didn't respond she was already asleep. It was that night that I told myself I would ask her for help in learning to fight. I had a feeling we'd be crossing paths with many more Kelsairans, and I needed to at least be able to help her. When she was fast asleep, I finally pulled my t-shirt over her head and got ready to sleep myself.

Chapter 10

Kheda woke me the next morning in a pleasant mood, and it surprised me. I expected she'd have a hangover. She looked down at me, and something was different. I rubbed the sleep from my eyes and tried to make my sluggish brain work. "You hate it don't you?" she asked. Finally, I figured it out her hair was brown with a hint of red.

"No, I just have a terrible headache. I thought you'd be the same way." I sat up an rubbed my head.

Kheda shook her head, "Kelsairans don't get hangovers. Do you like it then?"

"You look lovely, but I didn't think Kelsairans dyed their hair either."

"We don't. This is my natural color." She saw that I was confused. "I bleached it many of us do in the army. It breeds superstition, or at least the government says it does."

"Maybe I should check to be sure it matches," I said suggestively.

"Matches what?" She had no idea what I meant.

"The rest of your hair."

"I never touched my eyebrows." She thought a moment and smiled. "Jackson, I don't have hair there. Only males do, is it different with humans?"

"Apparently."

"Now I know you were behaving on Micea. Do you want to see?"

"No, I already have enough problems keeping my imagination in check." I was frustrated, and I didn't mean for her to see, but she did just the same.

She sat down beside me on the bed. "I will marry you soon, Jackson, I promise. Can I do anything in the meantime?" I couldn't believe she was asking me this. Apparently, she and her aunt had more than a chat. For some reason, though, I couldn't ask anything of her.

"No, I'm fine really."

"Jackson, I wouldn't mind," she started, and I stopped her. There was something about the fact that she was still a virgin that bothered me. I wanted her to stay innocent until she was ready not change because she knew I was getting frustrated. Besides, this was the woman I decided to spend the rest of my life with; I didn't want her doing anything she'd regret or even dislike later in life. "All right then; we should get started on your hair."

"What are you doing to my hair?"

"I thought you'd like to be the blond for a while." I looked at her a moment and then realized she had a point. Our descriptions, if not our pictures, would be everywhere. Finally, I relented and got out of bed.

It took nearly an hour for her to bleach my hair and give it a quick trim. When I finally thought she was through it, she pulled out two small round plastic cases. "What are you doing now?" I asked, getting worried.

"You can't go to Vali as a human."

"I'm good enough to marry but not be seen in public with?" I grabbed her and pulled her into my lap.

"Jackson, it's a necessity. The shape modulator will only change your form. It can't change coloring." I unscrewed the lid and saw two opaque blue discs inside.

"What are those?"

"They will change your eye color. Ceron's have unique eyes and your build and coloring is close enough."

"They go in my eyes?" I set her back on her feet.

"Of course," She smiled.

I held her at arm's length, "Kheda, I don't know."

She went to the sink and washed her hands. "Just tilt your head back and hold still." I did as she asked and she put one of the discs in my eye.

"It stings." I jumped.

"Baby," She scolded, "just give it a second." I blinked a few times, and it didn't bother me anymore. As a matter of fact, I didn't even know it was there. "Now the other." She put the other in and it wasn't as bad. Then she switched on the shape modulator. My skin tingled. It didn't really change one's shape just altered the light field around it to give the appearance that it had. Kheda's unit was expensive and likely government issued. She looked from this angle and that and even dragged me outside before she was satisfied. Then she handed me a mirror. "Well, what do you think?"

I couldn't believe my eyes. I wouldn't have recognized myself. I doubt even my parents would. "Impressive."

"Will you load up the cruiser while I get ready? I'll leave new clothes out for you when you're done." She said, heading back to the bedroom.

I loaded the cruiser, cleaned the kitchen, and made the house look as if no one had been here. Still, she was not ready. I changed in the downstairs bathroom and threw my other clothes into my bag. I hated the clothes she picked for me. A crimson Kelsairan shirt with black and gold trim and pants to match. She even managed to find just as pretentious black shoes. I suppose she had a good reason though and put them on without a fuss. Kheda was just coming downstairs when I came inside.

She wore a blue, low-cut dress that looked like it was made of strips of fabric rather than one piece. There were no real sleeves, just pieces of fabric gathered at her wrist. She had on matching heels that laced partly up her calf. Her hair hung in soft curls around her face and she wore makeup for the first time that I could remember. It wasn't overwhelming, but enough to enhance her delicate facial features. I was speechless as I got to my feet. If I hadn't already proposed to her, I would have done so then.

"God, you're the most beautiful thing I've ever seen." Was all I could manage. It didn't feel like enough, but she blushed. She walked by, and I could smell her perfume. I followed her out the door like a lost puppy. I helped her into the cruiser after she'd locked the door. It was stupid, I know. This was a woman who could beat me in a fair fight, but suddenly she seemed much more than that. She was my equal to be sure but also a woman at the height of her beauty and femininity. She pulled a scarf over her hair as I climbed in.

"You look very handsome, Jackson, but I prefer you the way you were."

"That's reassuring since this is only temporary."

"Tonight my name is Cia. It's a pet name my brother will recognize but no one else will. He made it no secret what I did for him. You shouldn't go by Jackson either."

"Then what would you call me?"Kheda whispered a name in my ear. I won't repeat it. She still calls me by it from time to time, and that name is between no one but man and wife. I gave her an earnest look. "I think Eli will be just fine.." From the way you talk you'd think you want your brother to kill me?

"Aya is harmless." She waved it off.

"Not according to Uncle Tam." I started the engine and pulled off.

She led me to Vali and once we were within sight of the city. I slowed the cruiser to a reasonable pace. The city was huge and built of gleaming white stone. The evening sun bounced off it, giving it a warm golden glow. Air and ground cruisers ran to and fro as people rushed about their business. Kheda led us through the maze of streets to the Theatre. A grand building that stretched skyward and was capped by a gleaming grey metal dome. Figures of Kelsairans and beasts that I did not recognize graced the exterior in exotic scenes. We parked the cruiser in a lot with many others and paid the fee before Kheda pulled me off to a small restaurant.

We found a table in the corner and had a quick meal before the show. Uncle Tam got us tickets, so we didn't have to worry about that. The waitress eyed me over and smiled, but one look from Kheda and she backed off. Apparently, it wasn't as rare as I thought to have a Ceron on Kelsair. I mentioned it to Kheda, but she said if they were anywhere on Kelsair it would be here, Vali was a melting pot of many different classes of Kelsairans.

I wanted to get a look around the theatre, but once inside, Kheda led me to the stage entrance. She told the woman at the door her name, that she was a dancer from the south, and that Aya would want to see her. The woman asked who I was and Kheda said I was her bodyguard. The woman nodded and disappeared. I could see part of the lobby from where we stood. The carpets were a vibrant blue with gold sunbursts. Strange winged creatures held up the wall sconces made of iridescent glass. And the massive chandelier matched.

The woman returned a few minutes later. "He will see you at intermission." The woman huffed.

"Let's get to our seats." Kheda pulled me along. We found our seats in the middle of the lower tier, and no one took notice as we slipped in. The lights were already dimming. "I don't know if you're going to like this."

"Why, it's just music."

"It's Kelsairan opera." I cringed at the thought as the curtains were pulled back. A man and a woman stood on stage with a strange instrument between them. Aya sat behind the instrument and began to play. The woman sang first, and Aya soon followed. It was a haunting melody and, despite the fact that I spoke the language, I understood very little of what was being said. I sat back and merely enjoyed the show. The woman left for the next two songs but came back just before intermission. Kheda got up before that last song was finished and I didn't want to go. She smacked my knee, and I got up.

We waited at the stage door for the woman to let us in. She came out just as the lights came up and seemed somewhat irritated. Kheda moved through the door, but the woman tried to stop me. Kheda looked at the woman "Where I go he goes, if Aya wants to see me then he comes." The woman huffed again and stepped aside.

"Just keep your visit brief; this is a big show for him."

Once we were in Aya's dressing room and the door was closed, I looked to Kheda. "What was all that about?"

"Looks like someone doesn't like my brother's dabbling, especially not at intermission."

"Then I guess someone isn't doing as Kelta asks."

Kheda looked to the door as it opened. "Apparently not." Aya stepped into the room and could have been Kheda's twin. He was a little bigger but if Kheda were a man he's precisely what she would have looked like. She ran to embrace him.

"Cia, indeed." He squeezed her tight. Aya glanced up at me and did a double take. "What are you playing at Kheda?" She looked at him. "Since when do you keep company with Cerons?"

"He's human." She relented, and he let her go.

Aya sighed, "Then it's true you're in a lot of trouble."

"I am," Kheda returned to my side and took my hand.

Aya sighed and sat down in a chair "Why have you come, Kheda? This is dangerous for me."

"Who else can I go to?" Her shoulders sagged.

"Did you have to bring your alien lover to flaunt in front of me?" Aya asked. Kheda crossed the room and smacked him hard. He remained seated as he stared at her.

She pointed a finger in his face, "You listen to me, Aya. Despite everything you may have heard I have remained true to Kelta. I am pure. He has done nothing to change that and has even denied me his bed."

Aya looked to me "Is it true?" I nodded "Why?"

"Because I love her." It was the pure and brutal truth.

"Kheda, what a mess. What do you want from me?" he got up to pace.

"I want the ship I gave you and some money." She put her hands on her hips.

"I love that ship." Aya stopped pacing to stare at her.

"Have I ever asked anything of you?" She folded her arms.

"No, you're right as always." He smiled at his sister "You look great."

"Thank you, Aya." Kheda relaxed once more.

"Come back after the show I will get you what you need. And Kheda, I hope you locked the door at my house."

"Of course I did, but you shouldn't have given me the combination if I wasn't allowed to go there."

"And what if I had been there?" Aya asked.

"I know your habits, brother. When in Vali you stay with Thris."

"And just how do you know this?" His brows furrowed.

"Special Ops." She smiled.

"God, I missed you." He hugged her again just as someone knocked on his door. I went out first, and Kheda followed.

Aya stuck his head out. "Miss Soloion would you be so kind as to escort Cia back to her seat and be sure she finds her way back here after the show. Send flowers to Thris and tell her I'll be back a little late."

We sat through the rest of the show and left just after the last song. Kheda was sure he'd have one or two curtain calls, so we had plenty of time to get backstage without being noticed. Miss Soloion met us halfway and grumbled the entire way back. She let us into his dressing room and closed the door after us. Aya came in a few minutes later and lounged in a chair. "Well, what did you think, human?"

"I have a name," Aya looked at me expectantly. "It's Jackson Peterson, and I liked it very much, although you went flat halfway through your second aria." Aya looked like he was going to tear my head off for a moment and then he started to laugh.

"Surprised you noticed. That took a lot of courage to say to me."

"You wouldn't be the first Kelsairan to beat the crap out of me."

"No, I suppose not." He got up from his seat "All right Jackson, I'm Aya; nice to meet you. It seems I owe you for helping my sister escape Kras."

"We helped each other," I told him, and Aya nodded in acknowledgment.

"Now, where's my ship?" Kheda was eager to go.

"My ship you gave it to me, and I'll want it back." Aya corrected.

"Talk to Jackson, he's a better pilot than I am."

"A better pilot than Kheda? I thought I'd heard it all." Aya looked at me surprised. "You bring her back in one piece."

"Whatever damage is done Kheda can fix." I looked at her.

Aya sighed "She's in the hotel hanger. The code's the same." Aya went to the wall and opened a safe. He pulled out a handful of credits and handed them to his sister.

"Aya, I can't take this; it's too much."

"Take it that's less than a weeks pay. Besides, without you, I wouldn't have it." He hugged her. She slipped the money into a bag that matched her dress. "Take care, Kheda, and try to stay out of trouble." She nodded and went out the door I moved to follow, but Aya stopped me. "What's your part in all this? I'm assuming you're Jeep but why come here?"

"I told you; I love her."

"And exactly what are your intentions towards my sister?"

"I asked her to marry me two nights ago." Aya was stunned. I wasn't sure if he was going to hug me or deck me, but he finally nodded.

"I know she agreed or she wouldn't have gotten so angry with me. I can only imagine what you two have been through together and I truly hope you can make it work." Aya went back to the safe and pulled out a box. He brought it over and handed it to me. "Take this." I opened it and was surprised to see jewelry. A green and gold necklace that seemed a little stiff.

"What is it?"

"For your wedding, men give them to women as a symbol of their marriage. I bought it for Thris but she saw one somewhere else, and now I'm having one custom made. Just don't tell my sister."

"Shouldn't I pick one out?"

"If you have the opportunity you won't hurt my feelings. At least this will give you an idea or something to fall back on." I nodded.

"Thanks, Aya." I headed for the door.

"Jackson, I'm going to have to tell Thris."

"I understand. We're leaving tomorrow."

"For a human, you're not so bad."

"The same to you, oh and your uncle's cruiser is in the lot behind the opera house." I pocketed the necklace and tossed him the box.

Chapter 11

We picked up the ship and packed our few bags inside before heading to the lake house. It was late by the time we reached it, but Kheda insisted we take a walk at least part way around it. She carried her shoes in one hand and held my hand in the other. It reminded me so much of Micea. I asked her about the ship as we headed back. I knew it was a human craft and nearly 30 years old, but I had no idea how she'd gotten it. It was built for long trips in space.

She said she found it at a scrap yard and bought it. It cost her three months wages and Aya countless more money for her to fix it. But she insisted it was for the sheer love of repairing it that she did it. She said she'd modified and upgraded the engines and changed the beacon code. So the ship, for all practical purposes, was unregistered. No wonder she wanted it so badly. Knowing her work, too, it was bound to be fast.

We went inside for our last good night's sleep together, at least for a while. She led me up a floating staircase that came out of a wall of windows to the upper floor. There were four bedrooms upstairs. We went through the last door, and I was surprised to see pictures of her and her family. "Was this your room growing up?"

"My favorite. We came here every summer." I wandered around her room glancing at the different pictures. "How old were you here?" I held up one of her and a trophy.

" 12, I won a sharpshooter competition. By then, I'd already decided to join the army in my brother's place." She had medals and pictures of her and her family in all sorts of competitions. There was one picture, though, that seemed out of place. A little girl in a red Kelsairan gown and too much makeup wearing jewels. "What's this?" I asked.

"Give it back." She reached for it.

"I just asked a question."

"I won a pageant when I was a girl, all right?"

"You won a beauty pageant?"

"It wasn't."

"It was."

"My mother's idea." She said, snatching away the photo.

"I think it's great. Who would have guessed?" I teased as I held her close.

"That was 30 years ago."

"30? But you were what, five then?"

"I was six, Jackson; I'm 36. Didn't you know? I joined the army when I was 21 and have been in for 15 years."

"But you don't look…"

"Of course not, Kelsairans live longer than humans. How old are you, anyway?"

"26 I joined when I was 18."

"Ten years; is that a problem?"

"No, I just didn't realize."

"Let's go to sleep. We need to get an early start."

"Just promise that you won't lose that dress."

"I won't now let's get those lenses out."

I was human again the following morning. Kheda packed the supplies to change me back neatly with her makeup. I made some coffee to drink as I began to pack the ship and took the first load out. The interior wasn't what I was expecting. Last night, I'd only seen the cockpit, and it was bare essentials, but the rest of the ship was lavish. The bedroom had a large bed and even drawers for storage. The covers were soft, and there were plenty of pillows. The bathroom had plenty of light and an artificial plant. The kitchen was no less homey. The table had a tablecloth, and the flat steel doors on the cabinets had been changed out with glass. There was a cooling unit for fresh food and even a range which was a luxury on a small ship. There was no doubt that Aya was used to a comfortable lifestyle. I'd be sure he wouldn't get this back for a while; he owed his sister that much.

I brought in the next load as Kheda ate her breakfast. I went in to eat mine as she opened the floor-safe downstairs. I looked around the open room. Two massive sofas sat on exotic rock floors that were highly polished. A metal table sat between them with a sculpture on top. That room joined the kitchen that had warm, red woods and green stone. All of the appliances seemed high-end, and everything was expensive right down to the knives. I finished my coffee and my breakfast before putting both our dishes in the washer. We waited a few minutes for them to wash and I put them away. Kheda already made her bed, so we were good to go. She closed the safe and put the rug back down.

"Did you get what you needed?"

"Yes, we should go. Thris is bound to be mad at Aya, and he'll tell her about us."

"He already warned me he would." She nodded, and we headed out the door.

Kheda stepped onto her ship and looked around. "Wow, what has he done to her?"

"Go look in the bedroom."

She went in the other room. "Aya's not getting this back," she called to me. I went in and found her lounging on the bed.

"There's time for that later. You still haven't told me where we're going."

She sat up. "To see a priest. I promised someone we'd get married."

"Well, then on your feet major. There's no time to waste." She smiled at me and got out of bed. She followed me to the cockpit and sat down in the other chair. She gave me the coordinates and helped me take off.

"There are few Kelsairans that will marry us, but this one has a reputation for doing so. That's why he's no longer on Kelsair. He started with half-breeds and pure blooded Kelsairans at home, and now he believes as we do. What difference race does make."

"They should make him your leader; that would stop the war."

"Priests don't get involved in politics." She was quiet for a little bit and then looked to me. "Can we stop at a trade ship? There are a few things we need."

"I'll see if there's one close." I scanned the area and found one nearby. "We'll reach it tomorrow."

She nodded. She sat beside me for a while then got up. "I'm going to the kitchen to sort through those papers do you want to come with me. We could reroute controls." I was going to object, but she looked like she wanted me near so I relented. I flipped the switch and sent controls and monitors to the kitchen.

She pulled out her journal and orders and set them on the table. "How far back does it go?"

"Fifteen years." The book was thick, and I was surprised it was paper. "Why didn't I listen to my father when he said to use a pad?" she huffed.

"What are you looking for, anyway?"

"I don't know anything to prove the war is wrong."

"Start with your orders and this mission." I found a spare pad and began making a list of anything we might need. Kheda read through her orders then started on the falsified documents they gave her. My list was surprisingly short, and I wondered what Kheda wanted at the trade ship. I sat down across from her an hour later and opened her journal. I flipped through the pages staring at the writing.

"What are you doing?"

"I can't read it. I just want to see your handwriting." I flipped a few pages further and found a drawing of a man. "I guess I wasn't the first to catch your eye."

"No, Jackson, you weren't. Are you disappointed?"

"No, because I'm the one you're going to marry." She gave me a crooked smile.

I flipped through the book more and found another drawing. "Is this your father?" She nodded without looking up. "And your mother on the next page?"

"You really are distracting."

"Sorry," I flipped through the book a while longer and came to a page that was loose the handwriting was different, and the paper didn't come out of the book. "Kheda, what is this?"

"Jackson," she started but then saw the paper. "Where did you get that?"

"It was in your journal." I handed it to her.

"This is my father's handwriting. He must have put it in there." She read the paper, and her jaw dropped. "It's a list of Kelsairan politicians, officials and even merchants with dates. It looks like there are human names with them."

She handed it back. I looked over the list and the human names stuck out like sore thumbs. Sean Masden was the head of a major arms manufacturer, and Trent Lacey was the senator for Sirus Seven. There were several other names I recognized, but I'd been out of the mainstream too long to know exactly how they fit in now. "Why are they meeting?"

"It doesn't say, but they do so every five to eight years according to this. A few of the names change but not all of them."

"How far back does the list go?"

She added up the years "Almost 70 years."

"Why would your father, put this in your journal Kheda?"

"I don't know, but he wanted me to find it." She looked up at me.

"Are you sure?"

"He never goes to the lake house anymore. He knows that's where I keep my important papers and assignments. The house was going to be mine when I retired. Aya got the country house; my parents gave the lake house to me."

"Kheda stop, we need to figure out what the list means. Is there anyone on there that will talk to us?" I handed her the list, and she reread it.

"Why is he on here?" She looked up at me "A priest he is a friend of the family; he's been to two of the meetings."

"I thought you said priests don't get involved in politics."

"I doubt he was in the meeting, but more likely he was there as a spiritual guide for one of the officials."

"Will he talk to us?"

"Oh, he'll do better than that. He'll marry us, too, I'm sure of it." She smiled.

"Well, what are we waiting for then? Let's go. Where is he?"

She sighed, "Last I knew he was on Aran."

"That's a wasteland. Why is he there?"

"To live in harmony with Kelta is what he told my father, but personally I think it's so no one bothers him," I grunted, wondering if he'd be happy to see us. I went up to the cockpit to lay in the new coordinates and find a trade ship nearby. The closest on the new route was a week away. But Aran was another week and a half past that. When I told Kheda, she seemed a little disappointed but said it was all right. "So what do we do in the meantime?" she asked.

"You're going to find a way to get controls to the cargo hold while I make room down there."

"The cargo hold for what?"

"Combat training. You don't really want to kick my ass in the middle of the kitchen, do you?"

"Interesting choice. I guess we would have had more options if we were married." She teased.

"You never stop, do you?" She shook her head "Then I guess the question is: once we're married, will you ever let me out of bed?" She shook her head again.

By the time I changed and moved around boxes to make space, Kheda had primary controls and audio fed to the cargo hold. It would be enough to warn us of any ships in range to fire on us or hail us. So far we weren't being followed, but we couldn't take any chances.

She came down the steps in a skin-tight black one piece with her hair slicked back. She checked for adequate space then moved in beside me. "I never thought I'd be doing this."

"I bet you've said that a lot since you met me." She smiled easily.

We started off slow as she showed me technique. It wasn't so different from what I already knew so I picked it up quickly. She made me practice the same moves for hours before she was persuaded that I was ready to spar with her.

I was nervous, to say the least. Not only was this Major Trekes but I saw her drop six men including two Kelsairans. She moved to kick me in the chest, and I blocked. She tried to punch me, and I stopped her. Another punch blocked, and another kick. It was all I could do; she was too fast for me. Then, I saw an opening and tried to kick her, but she dropped me with a punch before I knew what was happening.

Kheda offered me a hand up, and I accepted. "Good."

"Good. I didn't touch you?" I scoffed.

"But I only hit you once. Some Kelsairans can't manage that. We'll keep working on it, but you have to move faster."

"I'm never going to win a fight if I can't hit my opponent."

"And who are you going to fight, Jackson?" She put her hands on her hips.

"Someone has to have your back. You can't do everything alone. You may be good, Kheda, but there's always a chance they'll get a lucky shot."

"Always worrying," She put her arm around me.

"Kheda I love you. I don't want anything to happen to you."

"All right, then; we go again tomorrow." Kheda kissed my cheek.

Chapter 12

A week's worth of travel and combat training brought us to the trade station. By the time we reached the station, I still wasn't able to touch Kheda. At least I was able to try now without getting hit. She merely blocked everything I threw at her it impressed her, but I still wasn't happy. Kheda poured through her journal when we weren't training. Nothing inside it was useful. The only thing that we had the mysterious list. She got off the ship first, and I followed a short while later. I was sure to seal the door. I had the list I'd made as well as the necklace Aya gave me. It took several shops before I found one that sold them.

The Kelsairan behind the counter stared at me. I wandered around in the human jewelry, then the telaithan and finally ended up in the Kelsairan section. There was a blue and gold necklace there that I knew Kheda would like. I asked the owner to see a black one beside it first. He lifted it out of the case unhappily mumbling something. I eyed it over briefly and acted like I was going to walk away. Then I asked about the blue one. He brought it out not much happier. Then he really grumbled when I asked how much.

"Do you know what this is?" He put both hands on the case with an ugly scowl.

"A gift for the girl I'm going to marry," I said calmly, and he eyed me for a moment before calming down.

"This is a dangerous thing; my people don't like such unions."

"It's not up to your people. Will you take an even trade?" I pulled out the necklace Aya gave me and laid it on the counter.

His eyes lit up. "Where did you get this?"

"Her brother,"

"This is a finer piece than the one you picked. Come on, let's see what we can find." He waved me over to a different section.

He helped me pick out a necklace for Kheda that I knew she'd love. He took Aya's piece as an even trade. I'm sure if I'd have mentioned Aya's name I could have gotten more, but then I'd have risked revealing who I was with. The shop owner wrapped it in a small cloth pouch so I could hide it from Kheda and I went on my way. I got the rest of the stuff on my list and a few new shirts before heading back to the ship.

I was stopped on the way to my port by two Kelsairans. Both of them were taller than I was and wanted to cause trouble. I tried to move around them. They weren't going to let me through. "I have no quarrel with you. Let me pass."

"He speaks Kelsairan." One said to the other. I cursed, weeks with Kheda and speaking Kelsairan became a habit.

"We saw you go into Mor's puny, human. And we saw what you bought."

"Who's it for?"

"My girlfriend." I set down my bags and moved them off to the side with my foot.

"Human or Kelsairan?" One asked as he grabbed both my arms.

"Does it make a difference? Looks like you're ready to kick the crap out of me no matter what I say."

"Oh, it makes a difference. So, what is it profaning our customs or one of our women?"

"Neither," The one in front punched me hard in the gut, and I doubled over.

"I bet you it's a woman," the one behind me said.

"Maybe," he looked at his friend. "It would do the slut right to have the human tear her to pieces before he figured out she's not a human female."

"Maybe he's already done that," They started laughing. The one in front hit me again. I was ready this time, and the blow didn't stun me. The one behind me let go of my arms, and I dropped to one knee. I tripped him and kicked him square in the chest before the other had time to react. He turned on me and glanced at his friend who was fighting for breath. "Stupid human."

He lurched forward and swung, but I blocked and hit him in the jaw. I kicked him in the side when he was still reeling from the first blow, and he fell on top of his friend. "You two should learn not to pick on humans just because you can, sometimes they fight back." I turned to leave but stopped. "Oh, and thanks for the tip." I picked up my bags and went the long way back to my ship.

Kheda was waiting for me and looked worried. I moved past her handing her the bags. The necklace was safely hidden in my pocket. I went to the cockpit to prepare for departure, fearing the two Kelsairans would figure out where I went and follow us. I told Kheda we were leaving and she didn't argue. She sealed the doors and disengaged the docking clamps before coming to sit next to me.

"What happened?" Kheda touched my arm gently.

"Two Kelsairans wanted to start some trouble, that's all."

"Are you all right?" She brushed the hair away from my face.

I looked at her with a triumphant grin. "Thanks to you, I dropped them both in less than a minute. The only reason they hit me at all was that one was holding my arms behind my back."

"You could have gotten out."

"Sometimes it's best to let people talk," I said pulling the ship away from the trade ship.

"Hear anything interesting?" She gave me a sideways glance.

"I'll tell you later. Some things need to go into cold storage."

"I will put them away." She got up and found my bags before heading to the kitchen. I hid her necklace in a compartment of the chair. I was sure it would be safe enough until I could move it while she slept. She returned shortly but said nothing else about my fight. She hugged me and kissed the top of my head before saying she was going to rest for a while. I took the opportunity to move her necklace and hoped she wouldn't find it.

The routine was the same on our way to Aran, and the trip was rather uneventful. Although, Kheda and I avoided being too near one another. We both knew our wedding was getting closer and it only made it that much harder to resist the other. We continued combat training, and I still couldn't touch her. I saw a few openings but hesitated to press my advantage. I feared hurting her, although I knew if I kept it up she would notice; thankfully though she didn't catch on before we reached Aran.

Chapter 13

The moon was a wasteland of desert on one side and permafrost on the other. There was little vegetation, and I wondered how the atmosphere remained. Kheda said there was something in the permafrost on the dark half of the moon. She went into a detailed explanation. It was tedious and only fascinating to an engineer. I hate to say it, I didn't pay attention. I asked if we should hail the priest, but she said he disliked communicators. She located his home and showed me where to land. The ship blew the landing pad clear of sand, but it was quickly blown over as the engines cooled.

She opened the hatch and sent down the stairs. She pointed to a structure on a ridge, but I couldn't see it without shielding my eyes. I went back inside and found the sunglasses I'd bought just for this reason. Kheda thought I looked ridiculous but insisted on trying them on. She handed them back, shaking her head. Her eyes were adapted to the bright light, only in the last millennia had Kelsair become so green a planet.

On top of the ridge was an outcropping of red rock and carved into its side was a building. It wasn't anything ornate, but it was beautiful just the same. The windows and door were arched, and wood shutters stood open to allow in the breeze. I was surprised when Kheda led me around the back of the building. There was a small oasis with two fruit trees and a little spring. Various herbs grew in pots, and a bowl stood empty by another door that was open.

"He's home." She dipped a pitcher in the spring and told me to take off my shoes. She washed my feet in the bowl before getting new water and doing the same with her feet. She stood on a carpet just inside the door and smacked a bronze ring with a hammer.

A young woman appeared a few moments later with a bowl of fruit. She dropped it when she saw Kheda. "Major, I'm sorry. I was not expecting to see you. The reports say you were killed."

Kheda looked to me "They couldn't find us, so we're dead."

"That's good news, right?" I asked, not understanding the significance of it.

"No, because once they find us, they will kill us." Kheda's voice was emotionless.

"They say your friend murdered you and he is wanted by both governments." The woman continued.

"Great," I sighed.

Kheda gave me a look, and I was quiet. She looked back to the woman "Bhet, is Ren here?"

"He is. He would be most happy to see you. Your father has already sent word of his great distress."

"How long have I been dead?" Kheda asked as she followed the woman.

"Two maybe three weeks. I lose track of time."

"Uncle Tam will have called by now," I tried to assure Kheda.

"If not, Aya saw us; he will tell him their story is wrong."

"Did you ever think he is simply going through the motions, Kheda?" an old man asked from his seat on a purple cushion.

"Ren, am I happy to see you."

"Bhet, cushions for our guests then start on dinner please," Ren asked Bhet. She nodded humbly and pulled out two cushions. Ren seemed old but well taken care of. He was skinny, but not due to hunger. He was simply a priest who lived here as a hermit. His blond hair was cut very close to his scalp, and his eyes were opaque brown. Ren waited until Bhet was out of earshot before he spoke again. "Your father knows you are alive, do not fear. He called simply to be sure I was here and ready for you when you came. Of course, he was playing the part of a grieving father, but you know your father, Kheda."

"He can always get his message across."

"What brings you to my sanctuary?"

"We need information. My father left a list for me to find." Kheda pulled the list out of a hidden pocket and handed it to the priest.

He eyed it for a moment "Fruit, bread, meat; your average grocery list." He handed it to her, and I thought he was crazy. He caught my eye and nodded. "I know only pieces of what is going on, and I can tell you, but you will have to find out where to shop for these items on your own."

"I understand." Kheda nodded.

"There is something else, Kheda? Something you wanted to ask of me?" He looked to her hands balled in her lap "You always ball up your hands when you want to ask me a favor." She smiled then and looked to me.

"We wish to be married. Would you do it, Ren?" She looked at me then him.

"Yes, I think it can be arranged. Kheda, tell me: have you done as Kelta has asked?"

She looked away from the old priest blushing. "I have."

"I always knew you would. You had more faith than many others to follow your path. And after weeks alone with your future husband, Kelta will be pleased."

"Thank you, Ren."

The old priest looked to me once again "You have not done as Kelta asked." I shook my head. Somehow the old priest already knew. "Well, you aren't a believer. The purification will begin tonight, and you will wed the next evening." I looked to Kheda, worried.

"You do believe in a god, right, Jackson?" I nodded. "So you'll pray, and bathe and fast." I nodded, relieved.

"And while you do so, I will tell Kheda what you both need to know. What the government has done to both of you is inexcusable." He stood up and offered her a hand. "Come Kheda, we will eat."

"What about me?"

"Bhet will take good care of you." He struck a brass ring, and the woman appeared a minute later. He whispered something to her, and she nodded. Kheda gave me a quick hug before following Ren away. Bhet took me by the arm and led me through arched hallways towards the outer part of the building. The air grew warmer here as the sun beat down on the rock. She handed me a towel and told me to undress. She wouldn't leave though, and I could only turn my back. Once the towel was around my waist, she asked me to sit and wait.

She returned a minute later with clippers. "What are you doing?"

"Your hair is not blond."

"No, but it is black. There's three weeks growth there. Can you leave that, please?"

"Fiesty," she commented as she moved the dial. I breathed a sigh of relief when the first of the hair fell, and it was only blond. When she was done, she made me rinse off the hair in a shower in a nearby room. Then, she opened another door and made me go in. It felt like an oven, and there was little ventilation. She asked me to sit on the stone bench and gave me a pitcher of water. I was to pray or meditate until she returned. I sighed hoping Kheda truly appreciated this and thinking the other priest wouldn't have been so strict.

Bhet returned in what seemed like hours later. I still don't remember how I got through the time. But the pitcher was empty when she returned, and it worried her. She made me drink another half a pitcher then gave me a piece of fruit. I don't think she was supposed to. Then again I don't think she realized humans didn't tolerate heat as well as Kelsairans, did. She let me take a lukewarm shower before leading me to a room where fresh clothes were waiting.

I laid down in bed missing Kheda terribly. I knew she was near however not knowing exactly where was torture. I passed out then and came to late the next morning. I had a cold towel on my forehead, and Bhet was asleep in the chair beside my bed. I touched her leg, and she jumped.

"Oh thank Kelta, you had me worried." Bhet put a hand over her heart.

"First time you nearly killed the groom from heat exhaustion."

"I'm sorry; I didn't know." She looked down.

"I know," I rubbed my head, and she poured me another glass of water then handed me some herbs. I refused them. "Herbs won't work the same either." She nodded. "What's next?"

Bhet sighed, "You really love her, don't you?"

"Of course I do."

She looked away. "Now you pray, then after lunch, you will be bathed before the ceremony."

"Bhet, I won't tell Kheda or Ren." I put a hand on her arm.

"Thank you, but I must."

Before she left me alone again, I asked her to go to the ship and retrieve Kheda's necklace. I told her exactly where to find it so she wouldn't have any problems. She promised she would. When I was alone, I sat on the bed and attempted to meditate like I'd seen Kheda do so many times. Yet, it didn't work. I only started worrying about everything in our future and if we were doing the right thing. I decided finally that we were. I'd rather be with Kheda for a few days than live the rest of my life without her.

Bhet came back more quickly than I expected and handed me the necklace still wrapped in its pouch. "You slept late, so it's time for lunch."

"Do you want to see?" She sat down beside me, waiting for me to unwrap it.

Bhet smiled. "It's beautiful. I'm sure Kheda will be pleased."

"I hope so. I nearly got beaten by two Kelsairans for buying it," I said without meaning to.

"Is it really so bad what you two are doing?" She stared at me.

"Our people are at war, even you did not think I really loved her." She nodded finally. Bhet got up and asked me to make the bed. I did so without question and followed her to another small room where a meal was waiting. "I didn't know what you could eat, so I tried making our plainest dishes."

"Thank you, Bhet." I sat on the floor by the low table, and she left me to eat. All the food was new to me, but I tried a little of everything. What I really wanted, though, was a cup of coffee. As if Bhet could read my mind, she returned with a mug saying Kheda sent it for me. I took it, offering my sincerest thanks. She smiled and asked for a taste. She didn't like it. Before leaving she thanked me anyway.

After I ate, Bhet took me lower into the home and deeper into the rock. It was cooler here, and the walls were rougher. She led me to a hot spring and had me undress again. I was beginning to think it was a theme with her. I got into the water, and she poured scented oil over my head, rubbing it into my shoulders. I could only think of how happy I was that I was marrying Kheda tonight. Bhet handed me a rough bar of soap and told me to wash. Then, she stood back and made sure I didn't miss any spots. When I was clean, she washed my hair and told me to rinse it out. Then, she had me dip into another spring to be sure all the residues were removed. Bhet gave me my clothes and showed me where I could change and get ready.

I waited for her after dressing for what had to be an hour if not longer. Finally, she came to get me. She led me back upstairs to the oasis behind the house. Ren was waiting for me there, but Kheda was nowhere to be seen. I stood before Ren as Bhet disappeared again.

"Tell me, Jackson Peterson, is this truly what you want?" Ren folded his hands.

"It is."

"Our people marry for life. There is no way out of marriage and being with someone other than your spouse is a grave offense." He looked up at me concerned.

"I understand. I've never wanted anything more. I can't imagine my life without her. Just one night without her drove me crazy."

The old man nodded finally. "Sen will be pleased with your words." He hit the brass ring with a hammer, and Bhet returned. She stepped aside, and Kheda came out of the shadow of the doorway. She had on the same blue dress she wore to Aya's concert and the spike heels that made her legs look twice as long. Her hair was a little shorter and curled on the ends, so it flipped out from top to bottom. Suddenly I felt underdressed in a black t-shirt and pants. My shoes were missing as well. They sat neatly by the door covered in sand. Kheda smiled at me all the same though.

She stepped forward and took my hand. When I told her I was writing this, she asked me not to write anything specific about the ceremony itself. It is part of Kelsairan religion and not to be shared with non-believers. I respected my wife's wishes and made no mention of specifics. What I can say is that it was brief and I don't really remember most of it anyway. All I remember is Kheda staring into my eyes and knowing she would be mine for the rest of our lives.

I gave her the necklace at the appropriate time in the ceremony. She was surprised, to say the least. Bhet apparently told Ren I had one for her. She nearly cried then but stopped when Ren held out his hand. He gave her something and said a prayer in a Kelsairan dialect I did not know. She asked for my hand and offered a titanium wedding band. I smiled, realizing what she wanted so badly from the trade ship. I slipped the ring from my right to my left hand during the remainder of the ceremony, and it hasn't come off since.

When Ren said we were one, I could hardly believe it. She moved into my arms and kissed me. I never wanted to let her go. Then I remembered the old priest was there. Kheda took my hand instead and with a quick thanks to Ren led me away. I had no idea where we were going, but she seemed to. She led me deeper into the house and eventually to a set of stairs. At the bottom, she opened a door. It was a spacious chamber lit with dozens of candles. There was a bed on the far wall and a small table of food on the right wall.

She shut the door and stood with her back against it. "Well, what would you like to do now?" I asked genuinely wondering if she were hungry.

"After all this waiting you have to ask." She moved into my arms and kissed me as she never had before. She led me to the bed and asked me to sit down. She pulled off her dress and stood before me in only her heels and the necklace I'd bought her. Needless to say, things progressed from there. It took us a little while to figure out exactly how things worked best but Kheda was patient and willing to help. Being with her was more than I'd ever imagined and was worth the wait. She'd done right by her religion, and I'd done right by her. Now she was mine, and nothing could change that.

She lay beside me with her head on my chest idly tracing my muscles with her finger. "Thank you, Jackson, for making me wait." I kissed her in response. "Now that we know what to do, can we do it again?"

"God, I married a sex-crazed maniac. Just wait a while, and I'm sure that's not the only way it can be done." She smiled at me.

"You think so, then you should eat to regain your strength." She got out of bed and went to the table of food.

"You can't seem to keep your clothes on around me." I teased her.

"Why start now?" She bit into a piece of fruit and let the juice run down her arm before licking it off.

"Come back to bed." She gave me a triumphant grin. But she brought some fruit with her. We didn't sleep very much that night, and I had a feeling it would be that way for at least the first few weeks.

Chapter 14

We woke the next morning to someone knocking on our door. Ren stuck his head in a few minutes later and smiled at us. He said breakfast was waiting in the oasis and left again. Kheda kissed me and ran her fingers through what little hair I had. "I like the black better." She commented as she got out of bed.

"I didn't have much choice. Bhet wanted to cut it all off." I found my boxers and pulled them on. Kheda laughed at the thought of Bhet coming at me with clippers. "It means a lot to me that you did all this."

"I know, and you owe me so take it easy today." I teased her.

"What are you thinking?"

"I want them to know I'm so happy to have you, that you can barely walk." She threw my pants at me before finding the clothes she brought down yesterday before the ceremony. She pulled her panties on and stepped into a blue one-piece. She left it unzipped, just enough to reveal her purple and gold necklace. She ran a hand over the metal before running her fingers through her hair. She sprayed on her perfume and waited for me at the door.

I snatched one more kiss before going outside. Ren and Bhet were already seated with a bowl of stew in hand. Bhet passed us each a bowl before returning to her own breakfast. "I trust you both had a pleasant night," Ren said solemnly.

"We did, thank you," I said, and Kheda blushed. Sure, with me she was a fiend, but with others, she was still innocent. She remained a walking contradiction, and I found it irresistible.

"You are welcome to stay for another day or so, but then you must leave. I'm sorry."

"We understand."

"What is it you plan on doing today?"

"Jackson needs to learn to meditate." Kheda offered.

"I do?" I asked Kheda.

"It will improve your fighting. Once you are in tune with your body, you will exceed your own expectations." Kheda told me as if she were my instructor and not my wife.

"All right, meditation it is," I replied doubtfully as I ate my breakfast.

She and Ren worked with me all morning. They told me to think of only blackness and then one object in every detail. That got me into trouble on my first attempt. It's something no man with a new wife should be told without proper directions. Not that Kheda was an object, but she was the first thing to come to mind. I focused, instead, on a toy I'd had as a child. A wooden dog my grandfather carved. It was stupid, I thought, but it was simple and easy enough to remember. Soon I could see it in my head as if it were still in my hands. I could almost feel the grain of the wood in my hands. Kheda touched my shoulder, and it was gone.

I looked at her wondering why she stopped me. "It's time for lunch." She smiled.

Kheda gave me another combat lesson that afternoon. The moves were more advanced, and I began to realize she hadn't been using all of them on me. The only reason I was able to get close to hitting her was that she was holding back and making me advance one level at a time. We didn't spar that afternoon. She didn't think I was ready. I went downstairs to shower and change before dinner, and Kheda followed me. She grabbed me just as I was about to climb into the shower. "Wait, Kheda, let me wash up." She shook her head and turned off the water but pulled me into the stall all the same.

We both came to dinner freshly bathed and dressed, although we were late. It was worth it, though. A little more exploring led to other options and Kheda was grinning like an idiot. The fact that her calm demeanor was gone flustered Bhet. All she kept saying was 'in the shower.' Ren merely smiled as he ate his dinner.

That evening, as I lay with Kheda in my arms, I finally got up the nerve to face reality once again. "What did Ren say about the list?"

"I was hoping you'd leave that until tomorrow."

"Kheda, we should leave in the morning."

She sighed and got up on one elbow. "They were meetings held in neutral space. Ren never found out specifically where they went and the location changed at the second meeting. Ren was not even allowed to stay for the whole thing, most of the time he was stuck on the ship."

"But why are the humans and Kelsairans having secret meetings? Peace negotiations, do you think?"

"No, Jackson. There are merchants at the meetings: arms dealers, medical suppliers and I don't know what else."

"They're trying to keep the war going?" I was stunned, but when I thought about it, the facts fell in place. "God, Kheda, think about what we've resorted to killing each other with. The plasma rifle Dan had was outdated simply because each side came up with shielding technology for their people. Each new technology was the same, and then Sean Masden reintroduced the gun and bullets. Soon your side had them too only a little different. We thought your scientists reproduced them but what if Masden simply sold them to your people."

"It doesn't matter, Jackson; my people are developing new body armor to stop bullets."

"We have the same. It's been around since the 20th century." She looked at me amazed. "We've used it from day one. How long have the meetings been going on?"

"Ren wasn't sure, but he knew it was much longer than the list indicated."

"I need access to a human database. I need to find out who the other names on the list are."

"Can your friend Tony help us again?"

"No, besides I've already put him in danger once." I thought a moment. "I know who can help us, but Tony was right. Jeannie is going to kill me."

Kheda sat up. "Who's Jeannie?"

"A very old friend."

"Jeannie is a girl's name. Who is she?"

"Someone's jealous."

"Sounds like I have a right to be if she's going to be mad you married."

I looked to Kheda finally. "You're right, but are you sure you want to know?" Kheda nodded. "Jeannie and I met in the army. She and I were friends with benefits."

"Meaning you had sex with her."

"It wasn't quite like you say, but yes." I squirmed under Kheda's glare.

"And why are we going to see her?" She narrowed her brows.

"Jeannie was military intelligence. Hell, she may still be and not told me. If she doesn't have access, then she can get it. We need her help." Kheda sighed and finally asked where Jeannie was. I told her she was on Sirus Three.

"Lucky for you it's a long trip; I'll have you all to myself. In the meantime, you'll be too tired to think about her."

"You, my dear, have nothing to worry about." I pulled her back into my arms, and she settled in beside me once again. "Why do you think your father gave you this list?"

"He's fought the war as long as I can remember. Not in an open fashion, but more in a 'save our people fashion.' He always told me he thought it a waste of our most talented minds to have them fighting with the humans. He said he was sure it was the same for your people."

"Why hasn't your government stopped him?"

"Because of all the good he's done. Any animosity he's caused towards the war has been overshadowed by his good deeds and programs. Like Ren said, he has a way of making himself heard no matter what. Aya has been helping him just little statements here and there, but it's enough for now."

"And what did you think of all this?"

"I was taken from one extreme to the other. I thought my father and brother did not know what threat the humans truly posed. I pitied them and humored their deeds all the time making a reputation for myself doing exactly what they spoke against. I was good at what I did because I believed blindly in what I was told." She looked to me. "And honestly, in all the fights I was in, your people did nothing to dispel those lies."

"Because we were told similar lies." She nodded with understanding. "It seems both sides want this to keep going. Do you think the list will be enough to make them talk peace?"

"I think there's something we're missing, or rather something Ren is not telling us."

"We'll figure it out." I kissed her "let's get some sleep."

Kheda woke me early the following morning. She was already dressed and packing the few things we'd gotten out of our bags. I asked her for clean clothes, but she shook her head. She told me there was a sandstorm overnight and we were going to have to clear the engines before we could leave. Joy just what I wanted.

Ren waited for us upstairs with a light breakfast and two canteens a piece. He walked us to the door after we ate. "Thanks again Ren." Kheda smiled.

"I will send word to your father and let him know of your marriage. Your road is not an easy one, but I know you can do it. You were always meant to be more than Major Trekes." Ren said as he hugged her.

"You've chosen wisely, young man. Take great care of this woman, and you shall be blessed." I offered my hand, and he took it not quite sure what to do. I shook it, and he smiled. "If anyone could put a stop to this, then it's you two. I will pray you succeed."

"It could have been avoided if the humans simply gave back the Sirus System." Kheda sniped.

"Or if the Kelsairans simply admitted they had no claim to it." I teased her in reply.

Ren looked at us solemnly. "Remember that in every fight there is one person who is wrong," he looked to Kheda "and one who is right" he looked to me.

"Are you saying..." Kheda started.

"Have a good trip, dear, wherever you are going," Ren said quietly. I took the bag from Kheda, knowing Ren would say nothing else. It was time to go and who knew how long it would take to clear the engines. We pulled on our shoes outside and hiked back down to the ship. The sun was still hidden behind the outcropping of rock, and I wanted to leave before it came out again. Kheda went into the ship and made entirely sure there was no power to the engines before we started. She'd closed the flaps to the air vents before going up to Ren's the first time which was going to make the process faster. The sand though still seemed to get everywhere. She started on the other engine, and I helped her when I finished mine.

We brushed as much sand off of us before going inside and closing the hatch. Kheda laughed when I took off my sunglasses revealing two clean spots on my face. I went down to the cargo hold and pulled off my shoes, pants, and shirt. I didn't want sand all over the ship. Kheda merely had to brush herself off. Now I finally knew the point of her skin-tight outfits. She sat in the chair beside me as I blew out the rest of the sand from the engines. We took off and laid in a course for the Sirus system.

She took the controls while I went to shower and change. When I came back, she had a cup of coffee waiting for me. I sat in my chair, and she sat on my lap. "Bhet told me what she did."

"She finally confessed, did she?"

"You really didn't have to go through the ritual, you know. You could have protested."

"You're worth it." I took a drink of coffee. And looked at her. "So what's up with Aya and Thris?"

"What do you mean?"

"He's serious enough about her to tell her about us so he won't get in trouble and bought her a similar necklace but yet he's still dabbling as you put it."

"He bought Thris a necklace?" She stared at me.

"How do you think I knew to get you one," I told her about the necklace Aya gave me and how I traded it in for hers. She seemed happy that I went through the trouble.

"She allows him to dabble when he's not in Vali because he is Aya. But that will end when they marry, and he knows it." She smiled wickedly. "You had to endure one day of purification. Can you imagine what Aya will have to go through?"

"What about Thris?"

"He hasn't touched her. Why do you think he dabbles?" I shook my head, not really understanding their culture. "Thris is from a well-to-do family. She would never shame her family."

"Kheda, if you were a virgin at your trial, why didn't you simply tell them? You could have saved yourself. I mean, a doctor could tell, right?"

"I thought about it, but they threatened to make every man who ever claimed to have been with me come forward and testify in detail. Better to be humiliated once than many times over."

"But they would have all been lying."

"Jackson, it wouldn't have mattered. The doctor's findings would not have made it into evidence, but all of those men's testimony would have. My family would have been shamed."

"Isn't that the reason you renounced them?"

"Their circle still knows who I am. Things are bad enough for them now I'm sure. Although, the way the government told it, you were the ringleader and killed me when I was no further use to you."

"We have to clear our names. My parents already lost one son. They don't need to lose another, and I don't want my nephews ashamed of their uncle."

"First things first, Jackson; we take advantage of my being dead to gather information." I was getting madder the more I thought about it. We had to do something so my family knew I wasn't a murderer and absolutely not one who used women but we were stuck for the moment. We had to hide in the shadows, and that only made me madder.

Kheda took my coffee and set it aside. She turned on my lap to face me. "I like it when you're angry."

I woke up later that afternoon and found Kheda back at the controls. "Not angry anymore?" I shook my head. "Just let me know when we need to work on that temper." I looked at the coordinates and realized they'd changed.

"Where are we going?"

"Just a pit stop. One of my safe havens. I can link with some of the Kelsairan databases from there."

"Good thinking."

"What do you want for dinner?" She asked me like we were a typical couple.

"I don't care, whatever." I looked at her a moment. "I think you should teach me to read Kelsairan so I can help you."

"I agree. I should learn to read human as well."

"English," I corrected her. She looked at me confused. "I speak English. We have many different languages."

"Then teach me to read English."

"We'll start tonight, and you have to behave."

We started that night teaching each other our alphabets. For once I seemed to do something better than she did and breezed through the Kelsairan characters. She, however, complained every step of the way. By the end of the night though, she knew them all and what sounds they made. It was enough for a start, and we headed off to bed. Only one of us would sleep at a time, but she said she needed a break before her turn at the controls. Who was I to turn her away?

We stopped for less than an hour at an abandoned base on an asteroid. Kheda downloaded the files we needed, and we were on our way. We'd been studying for over a week in the evenings, and I could at least pick out names and some words. It was enough to run searches while it was my turn at the controls. Kheda could read what I found later. Combat training was every morning, and I never made it to the shower without a detour.

After combat training one morning, on the way to Sirus Three, I expected the same game. Kheda moved in close and kissed me a long moment before pulling away. "Go take a shower."

I looked at her, wondering what I'd done wrong. I felt like we were back on Kras. Perhaps this was for the same reason. I left without question, figuring she'd tell me what was going on eventually. I stepped out of the shower, and she stepped in without a word. Before she closed the door, I noticed the knob was set to cold. I got dressed and went to the controls.

Kheda came out a short while later looking miserable. "That's the worst experience of my life. How many of those did you take on my behalf?"

"Too many." I couldn't help laughing at her. I brushed a strand of hair out of her eyes. "What's this all about anyway?"

She looked out into space for a long moment. "Jackson, do you want children?"

I nearly spit out my coffee. "I... I hadn't really thought about it, why?" She looked at me a moment. "You're not, are you?" She shook her head. "Kheda, children, would be fine if that's what you want. I just don't think this would be a good time."

"Then we must resist for the next week." She said getting up.

I followed her into the kitchen "Kheda, I know you don't like talking about these things, but I'm not Kelsairan. I don't know what's going on."

She sat down at the table. "Kelsarian females of breeding age are on a seven-week cycle. They are fertile on week five and, if conception does not take place during that time, their courses come on week seven."

"So I guess it's week five." She nodded. I sat down across from her and took her hand. "It's all right, Kheda, just tell me next time, agreed?"

"No combat training this week, please. I can't resist you when you're all worked up."

"I noticed. Kheda human women have other methods of birth control. Don't Kelsairans as well?"

"You and I just don't have access at the moment. We'll have to be careful that's all. Aunt Sai has used this method for ten years; it's reliable." I nodded trusting her.

Towards the end of the week, I knew she was getting frustrated. I offered to help her, but I don't think she understood what I meant. Finally, I just carried her to the bedroom and threw her on the bed. She protested at first, but when she relaxed, she was a much happier and saner woman. I should have guessed Kelsairans had a higher sex drive than humans based on the way Salea and Teesa were always holed up together but it never really occurred to me. Oh well; I'm not really complaining. I'm just hoping she learns to pace herself.

We sorted through years worth of documents organizing them into files on each person on the list. Sometimes we were lucky and found information on the humans as well, but mostly it was all on the Kelsairans. None of it though was proving very helpful. I was beginning to wonder if we needed older records. I told Kheda as much, but she said she didn't have access. I only hoped Jeannie could get us what we needed from Earth's records.

Chapter 15

Five weeks of travel and research only brought us to the Sirus System. I was worried about stopping home, but Kheda insisted. She even cut my hair and put on my favorite dress. She wore make-up and her perfume too. I didn't want to land the ship. Then I saw my parent's home for the first time in two years, and nothing could keep me away. I only prayed that they took our marriage as well as Aya did.

I found a fallow field and landed the ship. It was close to the house, but the ground was soft, and Kheda wouldn't get far in those heels. Kheda just took them off when I told her. "At least you're not taller than me anymore." I teased her.

"Are you sure you don't want me to wait?"

"I'm sure. I know where they'll be. Dad will be on the porch on his rocker and mom will be starting dinner. Just hang back a little when we get close; they've never seen a Kelsairan." She nodded, and we headed out the hatch.

My parents were waiting for me on the road as we turned the last bend to the house. I thought I'd landed far enough away so they wouldn't come to meet me. Then I saw who ratted me out; Matthew and Gabriel, my sister's boys. I asked Kheda to wait and went ahead. I could see my parents straining to see her as I approached. Then my mother saw me and forgot about Kheda, at least for the moment.

"Jackson, we were worried." She hugged me.

"If not for your letter we almost could have believed those lies." My father said with a grin. "Tony got it to us just before the news hit. Said you came to his restaurant."

"You read my letter then?" They both nodded.

"Foolhardy thing to do risk your life for a woman."

"Kyle," my mother scolded him.

"They weren't going to let us out. I was going to die in there."

My mother turned away. I could tell she was trying not to cry. "We know, son." My father hugged me for the first time since I'd left to join the army.

"Is that her, Jackson?" my mother asked.

"It is, but I have to tell you, we… we got married over a month ago."

My father looked concerned "A Kelsairan, Jackson? And not just any Kelsairan, but Major Trekes? She's killed more of us than anyone knows."

"Dad, I love her." My mother gave my father a nasty glare. "things are going on in the war on both sides that are wrong. Both our governments have been lying to us."

"Jackson…"

"I know I sound crazy, but I can't tell you everything, for its too dangerous for you if I did. You just have to trust me." He nodded finally. "And Dad, just so you know, I killed my fair share of Kelsairans."

"Jackson, stop," my mother hated talk of the war. "Kyle, this was Jackson's decision, and he made it now we have to accept it. Whether Kelsairan or not, this is the woman he chose."

"Well, let's meet her then." My father finally said.

I went back and took Kheda by the arm. She looked at me worried because it had taken so long. I assured her everything would be all right.

I saw my father's eyes brighten when he saw her. There was no denying she was a beautiful woman. I saw my mother slump with relief when she saw my father's glower diminish.

"Well now, young lady, it's a pleasure to meet you." He said as if he'd been happy from the start.

"Kheda, this is my father Kyle and my mother, Saleena."

"Kheda?" my father was confused.

"My given name Mr. Peterson." She said in perfect English.

He was still confused but was more impressed with her ability to speak English. Matthew and Gabriel appeared from their hiding spot and stood before Kheda, staring up at her like she was a mountain. "My nephews, Gabriel and Matthew."

"Hello, little men." She said as she bent down to have a closer look.

"Are you really Kelsairan?" Gabriel, the older and bolder of the two twins asked.

"I am."

"Why are you here?"

"I'm married to your uncle."

"Wow really?" Gabriel looked to me. "Good job, Uncle Jackson." Both boys took a hand and pulled her to the house.

"Is Sarah here?" My mother nodded. "Crap, I'd better warn her."

"Matthew Gabriel, stop that. Go get your uncle's things from his ship." The boys raced past me towards the ship.

"Dad, we'll just sleep out there. I'm sure the house is full with Sarah and the boys."

"Sarah and Mark stay in her room, and the boys stay in Luke's. Your room is yours."

I stopped beside my father and held his arm so my mother would walk ahead "It's also right next to Luke's room." I looked away hoping he wouldn't make me elaborate.

"And ours, I guess you two will have to be very quiet." He grinned.

"Dad,"

"You're mother will be disappointed. You come all this way and not stay in her house? I'd never heard the end of it and neither would you. Do us both a favor, huh Jackson?" he pat me on the back.

I sighed. "All right, go warn Sarah. I'm going to keep the boys out of mischief."

"I'll go. I want to see this thing." My dad waved indicating the ship.

"All I have to say is her brother gave it to us, and he's well off." For some reason, I knew if he saw it without some warning. He'd think

I was lying or I'd stolen it. I don't know what I was thinking, but it had been Kheda's and my home for two months, and I was suddenly defensive.

Sarah looked up as I stepped into the kitchen. She stopped chopping carrots and let the knife go. "Jackson, I'm so glad you're home." She hugged me then let me go. "You look good."

"Thanks, Sarah." I smiled at her.

"Just in time for dinner as usual." Sarah turned back to the stove.

"Sarah I didn't come alone." I picked at her vegetables.

"Is Jeannie here?" She glanced over her shoulder.

"No, I brought someone else." I snatched a carrot.

"Who, Jackson?"

"My wife."

"You got married? That's wonderful but who if not Jeannie?" She stopped stirring the pot and faced me smiling.

"Jeannie and I were friends; we never planned to get married." She gave me a harsh look. "You'll like her, I promise; but Sarah, she's Kelsairan."

"Jackson, stop joking."

"Mom and dad didn't show you my letter, did they?" She stared at me. They hadn't, of course, so she wouldn't worry. "Kheda and I met on Micea while we were both on leave, we've been through some hard times since and well we got married over a month ago."

I offered her my hand showing her the wedding band. She sat down in a chair before nodding "Have the boys seen her?"

"Gabriel approves."

"It's just a shock Jackson you go off to fight them and end up marrying one." She got to her feet "Can she eat our food?" she asked. I smiled that was all there was to it with Sarah she was easy enough to convince. If I was happy, she was too..

"Who is this gorgeous young woman?" Mark asked as he came in the kitchen with Kheda on his arm.

"Jackson's wife apparently," Sarah said with a harsh glance at her husband.

"I tried to tell him,. I spoke English and everything." Kheda explained to me while looking at Mark.

"Mark just likes to make an entrance." Sarah smacked her husband's hand as he stole a carrot. He grabbed her and kissed her cheek before letting her go. "I'm Sarah, Jackson's sister."

"Kheda Peterson." She replied with a smile. I glanced at her not knowing she wanted to take my name. Sarah was amused.

"I like her," Mark told me.

"You would," Sarah replied.

"But I love you," Mark recovered.

"Keep that up, and you'll be in trouble with both of us," I warned Mark. He was a good guy really; he was just always smooth when it came to women. I noticed Kheda watching him and my sister. I'm sure it was strange for her. Sarah was only 5'5" with dark hair and eyes. She looked a lot like our mother. Mark was an even six feet and towered over Sarah. He had blonde hair and brown eyes but was tan from working on his own farm that joined my parents. They'd bought it from the Smith's when they moved back to Earth. It kept them close, and my parents needed the help with me away.

Mark and my sister had always been close and married young. They never hid their affection for one another. Kheda seemed spellbound by their interaction. The way he'd interrupt her cooking or get in trouble for tasting it. I always found it surprising they didn't have more children. But then again, the boys were a handful. Mark finally stopped pestering Sarah and sat down at the table. I sat down across from him, and Kheda sat on my lap.

"Staying long, Jackson?" Mark asked pouring us each a glass of iced tea.

"Mark, you know we can't." Sarah glanced over her shoulder as if it were Kheda's fault.

"The boys miss you," Mark said taking a long drink.

"I know, but it can't be helped when things settle down we'll come back."

"They'll be a new baby by then." I looked at Sarah.

"I'm hoping for a girl." She went back to her pot on the stove.

Kheda got up "A baby? Really? Are you carrying now? How does it work with humans?" Sarah looked to me for help.

"She's just curious. She won't even talk to me about it." I offered. My mother came in and took over at the stove.

Mark looked at me. "I guess because you're a man." I shrugged. I had no idea why she did half of what she did. Kheda and Sarah disappeared into the living room.

"God Jackson, where did you find her?" Mark asked quietly so my mother wouldn't overhear. "I love Sarah, don't get me wrong. I wouldn't trade her for anything but man." He shook his head looking towards the living room.

"It's a long and complicated story, just like the rest of our life is going to be." I looked to the door as the boys ran in with a bag a piece.

"Take those straight to your uncle's room and don't open them," Mark yelled after them. My father stood in the door and waved us both outside. He sat down in his rocker on the porch and tossed us both a beer. Mark and I leaned on the rail. Dad pulled out my letter and handed it to Mark. I nodded in approval. Mark set aside his beer and read the letter when he was done he took a long drink.

"How long were you in there?" Mark finally asked.

"Eight, almost nine, months."

"They can't do that you were a prisoner of war and they knew it."

"They did it to me, and they trumped up charges on Kheda." I took a drink. "there were other soldiers in there. They'd been there long enough to fit in so they wouldn't get the crap beat out of them every day. It happens more than anyone knows."

"You have to go to the government."

My father shook his head then looked to me. "Why are they saying you killed her? She's obviously alive."

"They want to find us and couldn't do it on their own."

"And our government is helping them?" Mark was outraged. I wanted to say more but I knew to do so would endanger them.

Kheda saved me the awkward silence. She came out on the porch and stood beside me. "Go put something else on so we can wash this."

"What? Everything is dirty?" I asked her.

"Borrow some of mine, Jackson. They're in Sarah's room." Mark offered. I straightened from the rail and finished my beer.

She smacked my ass as I walked away. I looked to Mark. "One hour and she's already learning your bad habits."

"Do you need help?" She asked in Kelsairan.

"No, I think I can manage." I countered in English to embarrass her a little. My dad chuckled and rocked back and forth in his chair. I found some clothes in Sarah's room and changed in my own. Thankfully, I'd left some of my underwear at home. Why I'd taken the rest, I had no idea. I was beginning to see the logic in Kheda's storehouses of clothes. I brought my dirty clothes back downstairs and threw them in a pile to be washed.

I found her on the porch with a beer in hand. "More bad habits, Mark?"

"She got that one from you." The boys came running out of the house and went down into the yard. They were pretending to shoot one another. Mark saw them. "Hey you two, stop that right now." He was off the porch and between them within moments. "What have I told you about that?"

"But dad, Uncle Jackson is in the army. We thought..."

"You thought wrong," I was beside Mark now. "fighting is not the answer."

"But Uncle Jackson, you..."

"I know Gabriel, but does it look like fighting is the answer? Is that what I'm doing with Kheda? She's Kelsairan she was in the army too, but we both decided enough is enough."

"The government said that..." Matthew started in his brother's defense.

"The government was wrong, both of them. No more fighting, all right?" I was exasperated to see it starting so early. They had a Kelsairan in front of them who meant them no harm and yet they would play such a game. "Go find a different game to play, all right?"

"I have a better idea. Go find your mother and grab your readers on the way." Mark countered.

"Dad," they groaned in unison.

"Can we have a lesson together?" Kheda asked the boys. They brightened. "I cannot read in English yet."

"But you're old," Matthew said.

"And I speak three languages. It's only the one I cannot read in." She corrected.

"We'll show you, Aunt Kheda." Gabriel offered taking her hand.

She let them lead her inside. I went back onto the porch. "Sounds like words from a wise man." My father said as he got up and leaned on the rail.

"Words of regret, I think. I was young and stupid when I left, and the only good that came of it was Kheda." I leaned on the rail beside him. "Maybe if I had stayed, then Luke would have, too."

"Luke was determined to go no matter what you said. You were the only thing that made him wait as long as he did. He believed even more strongly than you did."

"Thanks, Jackson, we've been trying to keep them as far from this as possible," Mark said as he came up the stairs.

"I think I'm only causing trouble."

"They try it at least once a week, whether you're here or not. Maybe now they'll think twice." I picked up Kheda's beer, expecting there to be something left but it was empty.

"Did you have to give her a full can?" I complained. They looked at each other. "Kelsairans don't metabolize alcohol well, and she's needy when she's drunk." They both laughed at me.

After dinner, I helped Kheda fold our laundry. "Those boys really look up to you."

"Yeah, I know, but they should look up to Mark."

"Maybe you should tell them that." She looked at the stack of clothes beside her "Jackson, I heard what you told your father. You should not regret your service to your people. You did something you believed in."

"I know, Kheda,"

"And you're brother's death was not your fault." I threw my arms around her feeling lost entirely. She held me a long moment before kissing me.

"Ahh, Uncle Jackson's kissing in the living room." I sighed.

"Aren't you supposed to be in bed?" I called up the stairs to where I knew they were watching us from. I could hear them run and then Mark's footsteps after them.

"Maybe you should let them see, better to kiss a Kelsairan than kill one. Perhaps then they will follow that path as well."

"Kheda I'm hoping there won't be a war by then." She smiled at the thought. "Perhaps then we could have children of our own to yell at."

"One step at a time, Jackson."

Chapter 16

The next morning I lay in bed listening to the sound of a busy house. I heard Sarah wake the boys and get them ready. I heard Mark, and my father head out the front door and the transport start. I heard Sarah, and the boys head out as well and then the screen door out back bang. Everyone would be out for a while.

Kheda kissed me, apparently hearing the same things. She moved into my arms and helped me out of my pants. I pulled off her shirt and threw it on the floor. She kissed me again urging me on.

"Jackson, dear, I thought you and Kheda would…" my mother started as she opened my door. We were caught, but mother didn't say a word. She closed the door and went back downstairs. I thought Kheda would be mortified, but she was a good sport she merely laughed. I was more embarrassed than she was. She kept assuring me we were married. I knew that was the case, but my mother just caught me having sex. Lucky for Kheda she was a very persuasive woman.

We went down to breakfast a short while later, and my mom was outside working in the garden. I poured myself a cup of coffee and went to talk to her. "Mom, I uh," I didn't know what to say.

"Jackson, you're a married man. I should have knocked." She gave me a grin. "Mark and Sarah normally lock the door."

"We thought everyone was out of the house."

"Is that why I slept last night? Thanks for the consideration." She put an arm around my shoulder. "She seems like a good woman Jackson I'm happy for you. I have to say I was worried if sex were even possible."

"Mother, I can't believe we're having this conversation."

"Do you think I've forgotten what it's like to be your age? Or what your father was like then."

"All right, enough."

"I'll come make you some eggs. That's what I came up to offer before." She said as we headed back inside. Kheda was seated at the table waiting for us with a kettle on for tea.

"All fixed?" she asked in Kelsairan.

"My mother's a fiend, just like you. Things I never wanted to know." I replied in Kelsairan. Kheda smiled.

My mother got out a skillet and began making us some bacon and eggs. "So when are you leaving Jackson?"

"In the morning, I guess."

"So soon?" She frowned.

"You know we have to."

"I know. Where will you go?" My mother asked with a sigh.

"We need information," I said simply.

"Are you sure it's wise to see her with Kheda?" She asked.

"I know all about Jeannie." My mother smiled at Kheda, and Kheda looked at me.

"Don't worry dear you mean more to Jackson than she did. They never got caught in the house and especially not in his bed. In the barn once but..." My mother shook her head.

"Mom, you're not helping."

"In the barn? Where they keep animals?" Kheda gave me a look.

"I can't believe Mark told you about that." I shifted uncomfortable.

"Where else Jackson?" Kheda asked.

I looked to my mother annoyed. "You and Mark are giving her bad habits."

"Really, Jackson? I'm just trying to be helpful." My mother said in her defense.

"Finally out of bed," Sarah commented as she came in. I gave her a look not wanting to get into it. "You forgot to lock the door didn't you?" My mother laughed as she sat down our plates.

"Don't worry. Mark and I made that mistake once, and it was dad that came in. I was seven months pregnant with the boys you can imagine the scene. Mark couldn't face dad until they were born."

"Where are the boys?" Kheda asked.

"I took them to school."

"Why are you guys living here, anyway?" I asked my sister.

"Dad and Mark are remodeling the house during the offseason." Mom gave Sarah a small plate of bacon, and she accepted it gladly. "I just wish I knew if this child was going to be a boy or a girl. I don't go to the doctor for three more weeks."

"The bio-scanners on our ship could tell you." Kheda offered.

"Really, you wouldn't mind?"

"We can go after breakfast. It's not far."

Sarah and Kheda disappeared for several hours after breakfast. I was starting to get worried, but my mother said they were probably off somewhere talking. I went outside and helped her in the garden as best I could, but more often than not I merely kept her company.

The girls came back before lunch and Kheda stepped off the transport with dad, Mark, and Sarah. "Where have you been?"

"It's a girl or at least it's going to be. We told Mark, then we went to town to get a few things."

"Did you go into any shops?"

"Jackson I'm not stupid. I sat on the transport with big oversized sunglasses on and looked ridiculous."

"I'm sorry, Kheda. One day I'll take you but not yet."

"I know, Jackson. I have a surprise for you." She took me by the hand and led me inside. She locked my door when we were in my room. She set down a bag in her hand and unzipped her one piece. She pulled it off past her waist revealing red lace panties instead of her usual white briefs. I was surprised, to say the least. She stepped all the way out of her clothes and turned around for me. "I don't understand why part of them are missing, but Sarah said you would like them."

I swallowed. "I do," I pulled Kheda in close and felt the skin on her bare butt.

"I have others. Do you want to see?"

"No, just keep surprising me like this."

"She wanted me to get something for my breasts too, but I don't think I need it do you?" I shook my head.

"Your breasts are perfect."

"If I'd have known non-army issued underwear was such a turn on I'd have switched a long time ago." She teased me.

We came down just as lunch was being set on the table. Kheda looked at Sarah and smiled. I gave her an approving nod as well. Mark was lost. I'm sure Sarah would tell him soon enough.

Dad and Mark went back to his house to keep working after lunch. I was going to go too, but Sarah wanted me to go pick up the boys from school with her. So I helped her wash the dishes and quietly thanked her for taking Kheda shopping. I don't know how they did it, but I was happy they did.

Kheda stayed behind when Sarah and I went to get the boys. She said she'd start packing our things so we could enjoy one last evening with my family. I drove the transport out to the same school Sarah, Luke and I once went to. The yard was already crowded with kids when we pulled up. Matthew came out to greet us, but Gabriel was talking to another kid. I whistled for him and waved him over. He pointed at me and said something else. The other kid punched Gabriel, and he hit him right back.

I was out of the transport before Sarah could say anything. I tore the two boys apart and held them at arm's length. "What did I tell you about fighting?"

"Uncle Jackson, he was saying mean things about you."

"They're only words."

"You're a coward then." The boy spat. "My dad served in the war. He told me what they were like; then you go and marry one of their filthy kind." Gabriel moved to hit him again. I freaked out. Kheda and I had to leave now. If this kid told his father, and he believed him, this could be really bad.

"Get in the transport, Gabe."

"But Uncle Jackson."

"Now." I looked at the kid, never thinking I'd have to deny Kheda, my own wife. "Gabriel is confused my wife is Telaithan, not Kelsairan." He wasn't buying it the kid was too smart. I didn't bother trying to convince him further. I let him go and went back to the transport. I told Sarah to drive so I could talk to the boys. I should have done it yesterday before they went to school.

"Gabriel, Matthew, I want you to understand something. I'm in a lot of trouble. Not for anything I did wrong or anything Kheda did wrong, but for things they say we did. Most of it is untrue." Gabe looked like he was going to say something, but I stopped him. "Most of it, Gabe, there are things you do sometimes to survive you're not proud. I did one of those, but I'm here.

"I love Kheda, and everyone says I'm not supposed to."

"Yeah, like Tommy Pearson."

"Just like Tommy, I have to ask you to do something. You're not going to be proud of it, and it's something I'm not proud of asking you to do, but we all have to in order to survive."

"Why, Uncle Jackson?" Matt asked. He was younger and didn't really understand what was going on.

"I shouldn't have come here. It put you in danger because I'm in trouble. I'm sorry."

"But we were all worried about you. We're glad you came." Gabriel offered. "We like Kheda too."

"Then will you do what I ask?" The boys nodded.

"Deny I was ever here. Deny you ever met Kheda or that you know I married her."

"You're asking us to lie?" Matthew looked at me confused.

"About this and only this." I looked away from them. "You have no Uncle Jackson until this is over, all right?" They both hugged me, and all three of us were crying.

"What did you do, Uncle Jackson?" Gabriel asked.

"Someday you'll know my whole story and proudly say I'm your uncle, I promise." Sarah looked at me concerned. "Take a vacation, Sarah. Go somewhere, anywhere." She nodded. I figured they'd go see Mark's family, but neither of us said it. "Sarah, I'm sorry."

"I know, Jackson but, the boys were right it was worth the risk."

We pulled up to the house, and I jumped out before it stopped. "Kheda, get our stuff let's go." She and my mother were seated in the kitchen; both of them stared up at me. "We've got trouble." She zipped her one piece further ready for a fight before running upstairs for our things.

"Jackson, be careful."

"I will. Mom, I'm telling you the same thing I told Sarah and the boys. I was never here." She nodded. "Go to Sarah's and warn dad then go with Mark, please."

Sarah dropped us at the ship before she left for her home. I was already taking off as Kheda closed the hatch. I knew I was being paranoid. I knew we had more time, but this was my family. I couldn't take any chances with either of them. Kheda sat down beside me, and I told her what happened. She rested a reassuring hand on my shoulder, but I wouldn't slow down. The race was on to make it to Sirus Three before they found us.

Chapter 17

It was only a two-day trip. Kheda and I took turns at the controls, never leaving them for more than a few minutes. Reality finally returned, and it wasn't pleasant. Less than an hour outside Sirus Three, four army ships approached. I jammed their scanners and long-range communicators, but I answered their hail.

"Identify yourself and state your business on Sirus Three."

"William Smith and my wife, Ann, on our way to visit friends," I replied.

"Turn on your view screen."

"Sorry, sir it broke three months ago, and we haven't found the part to fix her yet. The ship's old, you know."

"Then slow your approach and prepare to be boarded." I turned off the communicator and turned on the intercom. "Kheda, get your butt up here. I'm gonna need your help." Kheda came at a run without any shoes on. She'd been sleeping, I could tell, but she was wide awake now. "They want to board."

"What are you going to do?"

"We're finished if they board. I'll be arrested, and we'll both be handed over to the Kelsairans."

"Jackson, maybe that's what we want."

"No, Kheda; we don't have enough evidence yet."

"I know, but let one dock I have a plan. You have a feel for her right." I slowed the ship as she locked down the doors.

I switched on our communicator. "Ready to be boarded, slowing my speed as we speak."

"Copy that, ship one will commence docking procedures." I turned off the communicators.

"Wait till they open their hatch and can't get into ours. Then, we'll blow them off our side and break free. At least we'll only have three to deal with then."

"Kheda, that's a bad idea. If we can get close enough, Jeannie has defensive weapons. She can help us."

She checked the controls and frowned. "We're still too far out."

"She can make it. If we wait for them to dock, the other three will close in. I won't be able to break free."

Kheda was worried. "You're sure?"

"Positive."

"Do it your way." She strapped herself in and manned our guns. She brought up shields and transferred power from auxiliary systems. "I love you, Jackson."

"I love you, too, Kheda." I took her hand a moment before letting go.

"Deactivate shields and power down your weapons, or we will fire." Came the hail. I fired up the engines and pushed ahead. They followed and ordered us to stop again.

"They want us alive. They'll target the engines. Use it to your advantage, Kheda." Her eyes went wide. She knew these were my own people we were going to be firing on. The first ship fired, and I rolled out of the way. I pushed the engines further and took evasive actions.

They spread out on my tail making it harder to avoid them. I looped back on them to give Kheda a clear shot. She took one out as the other two peeled off. They came at me from either side now. The fourth ship that was going to dock with us finally caught up. Kheda took it out before it was even in the game. We were getting closer to the planet now, and I dared not push the engines any further. I sent the signal to Jeannie, hoping she'd respond. The other two ships were tearing my shields to pieces and Kheda couldn't get a lock. This ship wasn't meant for a dogfight. I sent the code to Jeannie again. I was going to have to slow down soon if I wanted to live through the landing.

I veered right, hoping to buy time and took a hit on the starboard side. Kheda got off a shot as well and knocked out one of the other ships engines. It was slowed, but it wasn't backing down. I was just starting to think Jeannie wasn't going to help when the other ship was destroyed. I looked to Kheda, but she shook her head. The other ship was hit again and destroyed as well.

Kheda powered down weapons as I slowed for a landing "They didn't get any messages out. I think your plan was better if not riskier." I nodded my heart still pounding. "And you really are a better pilot." Her voice was steady even though her hands had a slight shake now that the fight was over.

Jeannie lived on a floating base hidden at the bottom of a deep canyon. It was tricky to get to, but it was highly defensible. Her weapons were hidden all over the planet and hooked to her computer network. She was waiting for me when I opened the hatch, and she wasn't happy.

"Jeannie, I missed you." She punched me hard in the jaw and knocked me flat on my back.

"How dare you, Jackson. Gone for over a year; then, you come back like nothing happened. Not to mention you're being tailed by two army ships." I got to my feet.

"There were four of them."

"That doesn't change anything. Life doesn't revolve around you, Jackson. We aren't going back to the way things were."

"I know, Jeannie, that's not why I'm here." She glanced to my hand on her shoulder. She started laughing.

"Did you really get married?" She thought a moment "There was a Kelsairan on your ship." I waved Kheda out.

"My wife."

"Shit, Jackson. That's Trekes; they said she was dead." Jeannie's face went ashen.

Kheda folded her arms over her chest. "Do I look dead to you?" Jeannie shook her head. "For a human, you pack quite a punch to lay my husband on his back like that."

"God, it's true?" Jeannie groaned. "You're in over your head, Jackson. Come on."

"You're not mad at me anymore?" I asked.

"You know I like it when you're helpless." Jeannie smiled at me.

Kheda looked to me "I like her."

Jeannie led us into her home and base of operations. She sat us down at her table and handed us each a beer. "What do you want, Jackson?"

"Information that only you can get us." I twisted the bottle in my hand.

"What for?" Jeannie asked as she twisted off the top.

"We're trying to stop the war." I looked up at her.

"I think I hit you too hard." She took a long drink.

"Kheda, show her the list." Kheda looked to me concerned "We can trust her, I swear." I said in Kelsairan.

"I may be MI, but Jackson and I go way back," Jeannie added in Kelsairan. "You're not the only one who knows that trick, Jackson."

"Yes and Kheda knows all about us."

"That's history. When you disappeared, I had to find someone new." She grinned. Kheda pulled the list out of a hidden inside pocket. Jeannie watched her the whole time. "God, Jackson; she's my exact opposite." I looked to Jeannie realizing she was right. Jeannie was shorter than Sarah with big breasts and behind. She was fit but much more curvaceous. Her hair was red, and her eyes were green. She was more like one of the guys. She wasn't very feminine or graceful. Kheda was tall and lean with just enough curves to prove she was a woman. She was a trained killer but remained feminine despite her years in the army. Jeannie leaned down "How many times can you get those legs to wrap around you?"

"Jeannie." She shrugged and took the list from Kheda. She looked over it a moment. "What the hell is going on?"

"That's what we're trying to figure out. We're going to need as much info as you can safely give us and find us a safe place to work."

"You can't stay here," Jeannie said growing concerned. "As a matter of fact, you have to leave before dinner. If Stephen finds you here, he'll be pissed."

"Stephen?" I asked.

"I told you I found someone new. Did you think I was joking and he doesn't know about you?" She sat back in her chair.

"Jeannie, does he know about your work?"

"Only that I'm in the army." She took another drink.

"Bad news." I shook my head.

"Jackson, don't lecture me." She snapped. "I'll help you, I swear, but not tonight. I have a safe house built into the cliff. Stay there tonight and come back in the morning."

I sighed. It was her life though, "Jeannie, can you arrange a secure and untraceable channel?"

"Of course I can." She snorted. "Who do you want to call?"

"Captain Armstrong," I told her, and she shook her head. "Just do it."

"I'll give you half an hour to get up there." She said finally.

I found the safe house and deactivated its shield. I pulled the ship into the hanger and made my way further inside. It wasn't as pleasant as Jeannie's home. It was sterile and built for function. A bedroom was to the left, a kitchen to the right and workroom straight ahead. I went in and waited for Jeannie to patch the call through. I asked Kheda to remain in the shadows.

The monitor came up, and Captain Armstrong was surprised to see me. "Lieutenant Peterson?"

"Captain Armstrong, I'm glad to see you remember me."

"Of course I do. Where are you?" He scoffed.

"No, my location is my business." I shook my head.

"Lieutenant, we just need you to come in so we can straighten this whole mess out." He explained.

"I'm not coming in, and there is no mess to straighten out." I folded my arms over my chest.

"The Kelsairans have made heavy accusations against you." He reasoned.

"That's all they are too. Major Artemis Trekes is very much alive." I tried to relax.

"Can you prove it?" He sounded hopeful.

"Major," Kheda stepped out of the shadows and into view.

"This man has been wrongly accused of many things as have I. He was held in the Kelsairan prison Kras without your government's knowledge for nearly nine months. It was there that we escaped."

"You escape from Kras but how?" His brows shot up.

"That's not important at the moment," I told him.

He sighed. "You still have to come in. Some questions need to be answered. Not to mention you are considered AWOL."

"That's ridiculous. I was captured protecting my men." I was getting angrier by the minute.

"But you should have reported back as soon as you escaped prison." Captain Armstrong was disappointed.

"That really wasn't an option."

"Where are you?"

"Ask me one more time, and the conversation ends," I warned him.

"What do you want?" He glanced at Kheda then me.

"Call off your men and the ridiculous wild goose chase. I can see it on your face that you know you were being used. They wanted to find me to get Trekes back."

"But why?" He was frustrated.

"For the same reason, she was in prison, to begin with."

"I don't know if I can do as you ask." He told me honestly.

"I'll send you 30 seconds of recording, enough to prove she is alive and that I am innocent. You work out the rest with the Kelsairans. You want a bio signature I can send that to, but you have to guarantee to keep your men off our backs."

"Jackson, why are you doing this?"

"You told me why a long time ago, only I didn't believe you then."

He nodded, and I sent the recording and her bio signature before ending the transmission.

"What did he tell you, Jackson?" Kheda took my hand.

"That the war is needless and the fighting needs to end."

"But he's still in the army?"

"He tries to keep young guys like me alive as long as possible so we can go home to our families. He told me that when I signed up for my last term. It started just after I met you, I have two years left on this contract."

"Let's eat something and go to sleep." She could hear the weariness in my voice and knew we both needed to rest. As tired as I was, though, I lay awake most of the night thinking. Kheda tried her best to get me to sleep. I was just too preoccupied. I finally drifted off halfway through the night with her in my arms.

She woke me the next morning with breakfast and looked concerned "You hardly slept."

"I'll be fine once we get some answers from Jeannie." I ate my breakfast and dressed.

Chapter 18

We took a small transport down to Jeannie's, and she was waiting for us again on the dock. "You have to go back. Stephen didn't go to work. They announced that they were mistaken about Trekes and now she's a wanted woman again. Her face has been everywhere this morning and yours too. If Stephen sees you, then he'll flip."

"How can you be with a guy like that, Jeannie?"

"Jackson, don't start. I'll comb through the records as best I can and see what I can find."

"Jeannie, who are you talking to?" A man asked as he came down the dock.

"No one, Stephen; its fine." he kept coming anyway, and it meant trouble. Kheda slipped down the dock, unnoticed in the fog. Jeannie went to stop him. "An old friend but he's leaving."

"I'd like to meet him." Stephen brushed past her.

"No, Stephen." God, what was she doing? This wasn't the Jeannie I knew. The Jeannie I knew decked me yesterday because she wanted to be heard. This Jeannie was practically groveling.

"The man has a mind of his own, Jeannie," I said as he approached.

"See he's reasonable, Jeannie." Jeannie unreasonable? If this guy only knew what he was dealing with. He stepped closer his eyes went wide. He realized who I was. "You? But you're a criminal."

"If serving my people makes me a criminal, then so be it." I snapped I didn't like him in the least.

"I suggest you leave my house. I'm calling the authorities." He took a step back.

"No, I don't think you'll be doing that." I nodded, and he looked up at Kheda glaring down at him. "And this is Jeannie's house. It has been for six years. I helped her fix the roof and repair the kitchen." He looked to Jeannie.

"He did."

"Jeannie, you can't just stand by while they do what they want."

"Stephen, that's enough. Jackson is one of my oldest friends. I've never turned him away, and I'm not starting now. They'll be here a few days, and then they'll move on."

"Well, I'm not staying."

"Yes, you are, because if you leave, you'll do something stupid." Jeannie sighed "Come on, everyone back to the house there's work to be done." Kheda walked behind him, and she was enough of a threat to make him move.

Once inside I pushed Stephen into a chair. He wasn't a small man, but he wasn't as large as me. He was lean and about 5'10". He looked like some sort of businessman. He had grey eyes and light brown hair. He looked like he'd break if you blew on him too hard. Kheda sat down across from him, and I took Jeannie by the arm into the other room.

She was seething, and I didn't really care. She tried to hit me again, and I ducked out of the way. She tried another time with similar results. "Jeannie stop,"

"It's all your fault I was happy until you showed up." She turned her back on me.

"With that little weasel of a man?" I couldn't believe it.

"They can't all be you, Jackson. At least with Stephen, there was a future. All we had was sex and laughs."

"And both were great." Jeanie was an enthusiastic partner in bed. That's why we kept our arrangement for so long.

"That they were," she smiled a moment then stopped. "You're changing the subject. You march in here with her and turn my whole world upside down." She stabbed my chest with her finger.

"Maybe I needed to. The Jeannie I saw out there wasn't you. Since when do you ask a man for anything?"

"Jackson I... Who are you to say anything?" She huffed.

"I'm still your best friend, Jeannie. You decked me because you were pissed and with him, you beg. It's not you, and if that's what he wants, then he doesn't want you."

"Damn, I hate it when you're right. The little weasel had me cooking."

"Why, Jeannie?" I was genuinely baffled.

"I missed you, Jackson. I lost my lover and my best friend when you disappeared."

"Well, now you have your best friend back. Either straighten out your new lover or kick him out." She nodded "His house?" She laughed finally. "Now that you're not trying to hit me, can I have a hug?" She hugged me then and wiped her nose on my shirt. "I hate it when you do that."

"How'd the Kelsairan vixen steal you away anyhow?"

"It's a long story. Did you watch her trial?"

"I knew that was you, but I didn't think it was enough for you to marry her. Not to mention the tape was obviously forged."

"Well, she left parts of it out. And then there was Kras. Well, we've been through a lot."

"And I'm sure the sex helped convince you."

"Jeannie, she was a virgin until we got married."

She glanced back through the door. "You didn't? God, you really love her."

"That's why I'm telling you this. I want you to know I'm not doing this to hurt you. If I had someone else I could trust, then I would have gone there."

"I know, Jackson. you're making too much out of what we had." I knew I wasn't. It was always harder for her to keep it separate, but she'd never let me end it. She always insisted she was fine with the arrangement. Maybe deep down inside she was. Jeannie was a complicated person, and I know she had romantic interests while she and I were lovers. "Come on, or that wife of yours will get worried."

Jeannie went into the other room her old self. Stephen noticed the change. She was confident and playful. The radiant Jeannie I always knew. "Sorry, Stephen, lovers spat. Well, I guess ex-lovers anyway. It looks like Jackson stays, and so do you."

"Did you say, lovers?" I sat down on the arm of the chair beside Kheda, and she leaned against me.

"He's quite handsome isn't he?" Jeannie asked.

"I like her," Kheda said in Kelsairan.

"But you see I had to let him go another woman snatched him away. He said it's because he loves her, but I think its because she outranks him." Jeannie looked at us and smiled.

"Jeannie," I scolded her. She winked at me.

"And you're just going to let him and his new lover stay?" Stephen sneered.

Kheda moved to get out of her seat. He'd just unwittingly insulted her. I held her back. "That's Jackson's wife. I wouldn't forget it if I were you. To call a female Kelsairan a man's lover is a huge insult."

"How do you know all this?" Stephen stared at her.

"I could tell you, but then I'd have to kill you." Stephen gulped. "You may have free roam of my house as long as you promise to behave. Don't try anything or you'll be sorry I swear it." Jeannie put the house on lockdown and transferred all functions to her command only. Stephen wouldn't be able to escape or make any calls to anyone. "Why don't you make us some coffee." She said as she led us into her workroom.

We searched through records all morning first for the humans that attended the meeting. Then, she cross-referenced them with anyone else they had political affiliations with. Stephen brought us coffee and even Kheda some tea, but we never let him in the room. We didn't stop for lunch either. Kheda wasn't feeling helpful, so she made us lunch and brought it back.

We worked for another hour or so before Kheda insisted Jeannie needed a break. I looked to Kheda. However, she wasn't saying anything. Jeannie relented, and I sat down at the computer to read through some of the files she pulled. Kheda rubbed my shoulders as I worked. I looked up at Kheda when Jeannie was out of the room.

"What was that all about?"

"It seems Stephen likes the real Jeannie. Maybe things will work out for her after all." Kheda told me. I nodded and went back to work. Jeannie came back an hour or so later. She was unreadable even though seemed her usual self. It was just as well Jeannie returned Kheda was beginning to distract me. She got off my lap so Jeannie could have her chair.

"Stephen is making dinner." Her voice was a little shaky. I looked at her "Lover's quarrel." She shrugged and went right to work.

I went out onto the balcony behind the kitchen before dinner. It wasn't a place for anyone scared of heights. The door opened, and I was surprised to see Stephen. "So, you're Jackson Peterson, and she's Major Trekes?"

"Just like Bonnie and Clyde," I replied. He looked at me confused. "Don't you read?"

"How long have you known Jeannie?"

"We went through basic together eight years ago."

"And you two..." He trailed off. Stephen was asking about Jeannie and my relationship.

"Just ask what you want. She and I never hid our relationship. I told my wife. I was surprised to hear Jeannie hadn't already told you." I stood at parade rest a habit I picked up in the military.

"How long were you a couple?"

"We weren't. Jeannie is my best friend. We needed the comfort of another person from time to time to balance out what we had to do on the battlefield. So, instead of looking for people here and there, and risking who knows what diseases, we found each other."

"How long did that last?"

"On and off for six years. I last saw her before I left for leave on Micea. It was there I met Kheda." He didn't recognize the name "Sorry, that's her pet name. I mean Artemis."

He nodded. "I heard part of what you said to Jeannie about her not being herself around me. Why did you push her?"

"Because if I didn't, she would have grown sick of this life. She would have dropped you faster than you knew what hit you. Jeannie, well, she's exactly what you saw today. She doesn't take crap from anyone, not even me. She laid me out flat yesterday and tried to do the same again today. You have to take the good with the bad with Jeannie, but she's worth every bit of bad."

"What does Jeannie do for the army?"

I shook my head. "That's for Jeannie to say. It's her career and her life on the line should she decide to tell you. But I will say this: if you love her at all, you won't tell anyone we were here or that she helped us. You could unwittingly get her killed."

"Why would you come here?" He was getting angry, and my respect for him went up a notch.

"I had no choice, and that's precisely why she's helping me."

"You could turn yourself in."

"That would gain nothing. What I'm trying to do could save millions."

"What is it you're trying to do?"

"I'm married to a Kelsairan. What do you think?" I went inside, not really wanting to talk to him anymore. He followed me indoors. I grabbed a beer and went into the other room to sit down. Kheda sat down on my lap and asked what the matter was. She saw Stephen coming and said nothing else. She knew I didn't like him and she knew it was for Jeannie's sake, not my own.

Stephen sat down across from us. I could tell he wanted to ask me more questions. I could see the wheels in his head turning. He wouldn't say anything as long as Kheda was there. "So, uh, are you two staying in the guest room tonight?" he asked finally.

"Trust me, if you want to sleep they will stay elsewhere tonight," Jeannie said as she came out of her workroom. She shut the door and locked it. "Besides, if they slept there, then you'd be on the couch." I grinned at Jeannie. I could tell she was joking but he couldn't. "What do you think Kheda make him earn his way back or just use him to the end?" Jeannie asked in Kelsairan. She already knew what I'd say.

"That's entirely up to you. The question is does Stephen measure up to Jackson." She replied.

"I really don't like being treated like a pet of some sort. I should have listened to my mother." Stephen looked at us, lost. Kheda whispered what type of panties she had on that day, and all I wanted to do was leave.

Jeannie knew what I was thinking. "Is dinner ready?" Stephen got up and went to check on it. It was a quiet meal despite Stephen's effort to make conversation. Kheda and I merely wanted to be alone. We left as soon as we ate and I slept very well that night, and so did Kheda.

Chapter 19

We went back the next morning, and Jeannie came to the door in her robe. She let us in before going to the kitchen for coffee. "Where's Stephen?" Kheda asked.

"Still in bed. He called into work sick said he had the flu. I'm afraid I have a touch of it myself. I found plenty last night to keep you busy when I'm not around today Jackson. I restored your voice command." She said, leaving us alone again.

"She's not sick," Kheda observed.

"No, she's Jeannie. Obviously, the two of them have made their peace. She stayed up most of the night combing through files while he took a nap. She'll go wake him up when she gets bored. She'll do it all day today watch."

"How do you know?"

"She did it to me on more than one occasion,"I admitted.

Kheda gave me a dirty look. For once she was jealous of Jeannie and me. "You never had the flu for me."

"Kheda, as soon as we aren't running for our lives, you can lock me in the bedroom." She smiled,. Stephen wandered into the kitchen and poured a cup of coffee. He wandered out again without realizing we were there.

We worked the entire day with Jeannie flitting in and out. She always did her best work when she was happy. She even kicked us out of her workroom for a while. Kheda insisted we take the opportunity to follow Jeannie's lead. We locked ourselves in the guest room just to be sure no one walked in on us.

"Jackson," Jeannie called through the door and woke me up. I pulled on my boxers and went to the door. "I found something you'll want to see." I glanced back at Kheda, who rolled over and went back to sleep. I closed the door behind me and followed Jeannie.

She sat down in her chair. "I was digging through records from the start of the war. And found this." She pulled up the original trade agreement that signed the Sirus System over to the humans. I read it three times to be sure there was no lease agreement or tenancy clause like the Kelsairans claimed. There was none.

"Jeannie, you're brilliant."

"More documents stem from here, but I have to decrypt them. This was easy enough because it proves nothing bad about our government. The others are going to take time, though; I already ran three programs on them and no luck." She pulled up another screen. "Although, I did solve another problem. A safe place for you to work, there on the edge of human territory. A safe house built for MI. I've already started moving the files there."

"Jeannie, I could kiss you."

She grinned. "I remember a time you did."

"What does Stephen do, anyway?"

"He's a banker; his family owns the Sirus Bank." I laughed. "Thanks, Jackson. He's coming around and learning to accept who I really am."

"Don't trust him with this yet, Jeannie." I was worried about her.

"I won't." She promised. "I have a different ship for you, too. Its more maneuverable but not as fast."

"Kheda can fix that. But, she'll want ours back eventually." I told Jeannie.

"It will be here waiting for you." She looked at me concerned. "Build a good case before you do anything, Jackson. If they want this war, they'll do whatever they can to shut you up."

"I know. I've already left an encrypted file in the cliff house of everything that's happened to us so far." She nodded.

"Rest tonight and head out tomorrow. You'll have to stop at a trade ship. There are no supplies at the safe house."

"We'll take what we can and buy the rest."

Kheda and I scavenged Aya's ship for supplies that night and had them waiting on the hanger for the new ship to arrive in the morning. There wasn't much we'd need, but it was enough to make us stop at a trade ship. We had one more night of peaceful sleep before another three weeks of travel.

Jeannie arrived first thing in the morning with a brand new ship. It was exactly like the ones we'd fought days ago. Light maneuverable and built for trouble. Kheda saw my eyes light up and grinned. They were four-man ships made for reconnaissance missions and quick strikes into enemy territory and ready for a dogfight if need be.

"Well, it's going to be a little more cramped than what you're used to. However, she's what you need at the moment."

"Thanks, Jeannie."

"Get going you big lug before I miss you."

I gave Jeannie one last hug before she left in her transport. We loaded the ship and headed out.

Chapter 20

It took three weeks to get to the safe house on an unnamed moon. We only stopped at the trade ship for a few hours. With our ship displaying Jeannie's beacon, that's the only place we ran into trouble. Five Kelsairans realized who Kheda was, despite her disguise and surrounded her. They hadn't noticed me ten feet behind her. We fought our way out and ran for our lives back to the ship. I thanked Kheda profusely for her training. I escaped with only a broken arm whereas before I probably would have been dead. She thanked me for my help as well, since she couldn't have taken on five Kelsairans by herself.

We fixed my arm with the onboard med kit. It took another week to regain my strength in it. Kheda complained because it kept me from helping her unload some of our supplies. There were a few things we couldn't get with the problem at the trade ship. Luckily, we dropped off most of our purchases before they found Kheda. We'd just have to make due.

The safe house was just as utilitarian as the one on Sirus Three had been. But it was well defended, and Jeannie had the files there waiting for us.

We fell into a similar routine as we had on our way to Sirus Seven combat training, sorting through files and making love whenever we felt like it. That is when we could. We started getting closer to the truth, and the picture got uglier. I found my whole world falling apart, and Kheda was my only anchor. It was a conspiracy plot beyond what either of us imagined dating back to before the war started. Those in government saw to it the war remained an ongoing thing. There were contracts with arms dealers, medical suppliers, shipbuilders you name it was there. The same was true of the Kelsairans only we had less proof.

There were still a few key pieces missing, and it was taking forever to find them. Kheda and I, in the meantime, were enjoying not being on the run for once. We weren't looking over our shoulder, and we slept in the same bed every night. We'd been married five months and here three. It finally felt like we were a real couple.

Kheda came to me one night while I was still working and said she was going to bed. That was it not that she wanted me to go with her, just that she was tired. I was worried because it wasn't like her. I asked her if anything was wrong and she said there wasn't. I thought perhaps I lost count of the week. Just the same, I turned off the monitors and went to bed.

The next afternoon she was ill and didn't want to do any combat training. I thought for sure I lost track of the weeks. I lay down to take a nap with her and fell asleep in her arms. I woke a short while later with her sitting beside me. She'd been crying I could tell, but she was trying to hide it from me.

"Kheda what's wrong?"

"I messed up, Jackson." She was miserable.

"Kheda please," I couldn't stand to see her like this. "Tell me what's wrong."

"I miss counted somewhere. Jackson, I'm pregnant."

I didn't know whether to be relieved or severely worried. Although, I couldn't help being ecstatic. I pulled her down to the bed with me. "Is that all? You acted like the world was going to end."

"You're not mad?"

"Should I be? I admit it's not the best time," She started to cry "but it's our child, Kheda. How could I be mad about that? Besides, you're not the only guilty one here." She laughed a little.

"Jackson, there's three of them."

"Three?" I swallowed.

"Kelsairans release several eggs at once to compensate for low male fertility. I guess humans are more fertile than Kelsairans."

"Did you say three?" I was in shock.

"Now you're mad." She buried her head in my chest.

"No, I'm concerned there's a difference." I rubbed her back.

"How long do we have before they're born?"

"Kelsairan children carry for 8 months, but Sarah said humans are almost ten sometimes. So I don't know. If I had to guess, I'd go with the lower end and say seven months."

"Wait, seven? Kheda, you had your courses last cycle."

"I know, that's why I couldn't believe it was true. Yet, I have all the symptoms, and the bio-scanners confirm it."

"You checked while I was sleeping, didn't you?"

"I didn't want to worry you needlessly."

"Come on, let's go back to the ship. I want to see them."

Kheda smiled at me. "Look at you. You're happy."

"Shouldn't I be? I'm going to be a father. And these children will have the most beautiful mother ever."

"I'm telling Saleena."

We weren't sure exactly what was going to happen as her pregnancy progressed, so I decided to put in a call to Jeannie. She was absolutely going to love this. I set up a secure channel and hoped she was working. She came up on the monitor and looked really unhappy about being disturbed until she saw it was me.

"Jackson this is a surprise. What's so urgent that you risked calling me? You're not in trouble, are you? No one is supposed to know about that base." She rambled on worried.

"Jeannie, I'm fine."

"Oh well. How's the research coming?"

"Well enough," Stephen walked into her workroom and said hello. "I see things worked out for you two."

Stephen grinned and rubbed Jeannie's shoulder. "So what's up Jackson?"

"I need a personal favor."

Jeannie sighed. "I don't like it when you get that tone."

"I need more info, but it's for private use." I wanted Stephen to leave, but he wasn't getting the hint.

"For goodness sake, Jackson; I'm pregnant, not inflicted with a disease." Kheda pushed me out of the way and sat down. Jeannie was howling with laughter now. "She would have told him anyway." Kheda turned back to the monitor. "Jeannie, we don't know what's going to happen. This wasn't exactly planned."

"All right, Kheda, for you, I'll do it. Good job, Jackson." Jeannie glanced up as she ran a search. "The information isn't that uncommon. You just have to know where to look. I'm sending it over now. Jackson stop worrying; you'll work it out."

"Thanks, Jeannie." I smiled.

"And Jackson, congratulations. I'll get word to your folks. I hear Sirus Seven is nice this time of year." Jeannie cut off the transmission, and the monitors displayed the files she sent. I downloaded them to a pad for Kheda.

"Jeannie's right, stop worrying."

"Kheda, now I'll have four to look after."

"No, we'll have three to look after. Go back to work I'll make you something to eat. Then you have a wife to entertain." I looked at her unsure, but she held up the pad. She'd pour through it to find out exactly what we could and could not do as well as how her pregnancy would progress. We hadn't been together for nearly a week since she found out unsure if we should. Although she hadn't really wanted to be either. I returned to my work trying to keep my mind off other matters. When she came in that evening to get me for bed, wearing only a pair of black lace panties, I figured she'd found her answers.

Almost a month later, Kheda woke me early in the morning with cramps. She was uncomfortable and didn't think it was a big deal but had me get her pad just to be sure. She got halfway through a paragraph and freaked out. She yelled at me to get a medkit, and I went running. She threw the contents on the bed and couldn't find what she wanted. She started to cry. I pulled her in close and read her pad over her shoulder.

The cramps could mean she was losing the children and an injection of some Kelsairan drug could save them. But, we didn't have it. Both were possibilities, even if one were happening, the other might not stop it. She was crying uncontrollably, nonetheless. I carried her up to the ship and activated the bio-scanners. We'd lost one. I started crying just as hard as she was. After several minutes I finally got control.

"Make a list of everything you're going to need."

"Jackson, you can't. We barely escaped the last trade ship." She was worried.

"Kheda I have to. We still have two left. I don't want to lose them too."

"Jackson," she started but finally nodded. She knew I was going to do this, no matter what she said. "Will you at least go in disguise?"

"Anything to come back to you."

So, two days later, I found myself as a Ceron stepping onto another trade ship. Three Kelsairans talked a fair bit but never bothered to actually start any trouble. You never knew with Cerons what you were going to get. Half of the time they had a nasty temper to match their brute strength. I purposely had Kheda cut my hair in my old army crew cut, hoping they'd think I was a mercenary. It seemed to do the trick. I returned to the safe house with everything Kheda, and the babies would need without incidence.

She slept with the new medkit by her side. We didn't have cause to use it in the next three months. I bought her plenty of fresh fruit while I was on the trade ship and she was rationing it out slowly. She offered me some, but I never took it. Her belly was sticking out now, and she switched over to the dresses I bought her. I finally worked out all the pieces of the conspiracy and Kheda was appalled. Now the hard part was how to get the governments to listen without being killed in the process.

Chapter 21

We took two weeks working out a plan right down to the most minor detail. However, we were going to need help. Jeannie would be no problem. She even made suggestions to improve our ideas. The hard part was getting help from Kheda's family. Somehow she managed to track down her brother and set up a secure channel. A Kelsairan woman with long black hair and gray-blue mottled eyes answered the call.

Kheda seemed amused. "You must be Thris."

"Of course I am. If you're calling to accuse my husband of getting you in that condition, then you can save your breath because..."

"My husband is the father of my children. I called to speak with my brother." Kheda replied.

"Kheda," now the other woman was amused, and I was confused. Thris disappeared and returned with Aya.

"Kheda thank Kelta. We've been worried. You..." he started then looked at her "You're pregnant. Where's Jackson? Is he all right?"

"I'm fine, Aya. Thanks for your concern." I moved into view before letting Kheda retake control.

"When is the child due, Kheda?"

"The children are due in approximately three months. I'm carrying two a boy and a girl."

"That's great news. Do you..."

"Aya, that's not why I'm calling. This is a secure line, but we still have to be brief. What I'm going to ask is dangerous, and even if you don't agree to help us, you can tell no one."

"One question first. How's my ship?" He grinned, and I knew he'd help us. Kheda explained exactly what she needed him to do but not how to do so. She knew it would be hard to work out the details on his end and let it be. He asked only that we sit still for a week.

We called a week later, and he said we were good to go. Ren had already left Aran. So I sent out a copy of the list to every name that attended the last three meetings with an ultimatum to meet at the base on Micea or risk being exposed. I also sent copies to their contacts in both governments. The politicians that would attend the meetings were mere puppets. I needed those pulling strings to know I wasn't playing. They had four weeks which would give me plenty of time to get there and plenty of time to get Kheda to safety.

Everything was packed and ready to go when Ren's ship arrived. Kheda wore a grey dress, and her hair grazed her shoulders. The sides were pulled up and out of her eyes, and she looked so beautiful. The hatch opened, and Ren stepped out. She ran to greet him, and he smiled.

"Another generation to bring into this world."

"Looks like you figured out the clue I left just in time." Another man said in greeting as he stepped off Ren's ship.

"Daddy?" Kheda took a step forward "Oh Kelta, it is you." She rushed into his arms.

"Aya told me you were pregnant, but I didn't believe him. I had to see it for myself."

She took a step back then looked at me. She reached for my hand, and I came forward. "Jackson, this is my father, Sen." I looked up at him. He was taller than Aya with the same blue eyes, but his hair was darker and his features more angular. I don't know if he was more intimidating because he was nearly as big as Tam or because he was Kheda's father.

"Well now, Jackson, it's a pleasure to finally meet you. My brother and Ren both told me nice things about you. Aya seems to hold a grudge something about a ship." I looked to Kheda.

"He won't let it go until he gets it back." Her father was still smiling though he apparently found it amusing.

"I take it you have a plan to make them listen and not get yourself killed?" Sen asked. I nodded. "Good, you can fill me in on the way."

"You're coming with me?"

"How else were you planning on landing?" Sen asked.

"My ship's beacon code is human military intelligence." He looked at me impressed.

"But I have diplomatic asylum. We'll double your chances if I go. Besides, I wouldn't miss this for anything." I nodded finally.

"Kheda and your children will be safe in my hands." Ren volunteered. I hugged Kheda, never wanting to let her go. It was the first time we were apart for more than a few days since we left Kras. I kept wondering how I would ever get through this and why I was doing this. Then I felt the children growing inside her, my children and I knew why. I loved all three of them more than I loved myself. I had to do this for us and all the others like us.

"Come back to me, Jackson." She whispered in my ear.

"Just like we planned Kheda. , You know what to do if something goes wrong." I kissed her and let her go. Ren took one of her bags, and I watched her leave. "I'll see you again, Kheda. I love you."

"I love you too, Jackson." She called back as the hatch closed. I wiped the tears from my eye with the back of my sleeve before looking to her father.

"If her mother saw that, she wouldn't despise you so much." That didn't really make me feel any better, but I knew what he was trying to say. Kheda told me about her mother. No matter what Kheda did, her mother always wanted her to be the best. For years Kheda did that as Trekes. Then I came along, and suddenly her career was gone, she was married to a human and having half-breeds. I knew her mother's type; we would face them the rest of our lives. Her father obviously didn't agree, and it made things so much easier. Kheda didn't really care what her mother thought. It was her father's approval that was important to her. "Kheda told Aya you're a better pilot than she was. Let's see what you're made of."

I nodded and took him to the ship that Kheda spent months tinkering with.

"How'd you know where to leave that list?" I asked him on one of our many days of travel.

"I know my daughter. Something didn't feel right about her trial. I knew she was either being set up or she was on a mission. I also knew she kept her journal and her orders at the lake house. It's remote, familiar and easily defendable. I found her orders and journal just where they should be, but curiosity got the better of me, and I read her diary for the days she spent with you. I had a feeling then there was more to this than just her mission and was afraid she might end up in a situation like this.

"I know the Kelsairan government, too, and they would not be happy with one of their soldiers, especially one as decorated as Kheda, defying them. I offered her a way out, and she took it. Of course, you and she are helping me achieve my lifelong goal as well, but it is for the good of all."

I nodded, understanding where he was coming from. I let him read my journal up until that day and offered to tell him everything we'd discovered. He accepted the journal but refused the information. He wanted to find out with everyone else. After reading my journal, he offered to tell me what Kheda wrote, but I didn't need to hear it. I knew she loved me and that was enough. How or when wasn't really important besides when she was ready she'd tell me. I learned with Kheda that everything had its own timeline. She was complicated, to say the least, but she was slowly opening up to me and unraveling 15 years of layers she'd built up in the army.

I couldn't help but ask who in his family served in the army. I was surprised to hear he lost two siblings to the war: a brother and a sister. He said that loss was part of the reason Tam and Sai never had children. They didn't want to lose anyone else to the war. Sen spoke very little of his siblings, and I let the subject drop. But that led to a discussion of my two children.

I told him of the third we'd lost early in the pregnancy and he wasn't surprised. He said the same happened to his wife, Cime when she carried Kheda. Multiple births were more frequent with Kelsairans, but when one child was lost in the womb, they believed its strength is given to the surviving child. It was actually a good omen.

Sen asked about my family, so I told him about the farms on Sirus Seven. Then he asked what I would do when this was over, and I had no clue. I'd served in the military for seven years, was a prisoner in Kras for eight months, and on the run for a year. I hadn't had time to think about life after the army. So much of my life lately had been about just getting to tomorrow. I told him as much, and he nodded. He mentioned that Tam would love it if we stayed with him for a while something about him needing help at the vineyard. I think he was offering a job, but he didn't come right out and say it. I knew Kheda would love being on Kelsair, but I feared the trouble I'd bring.

I thought then about going back to Sirus Seven, but that could hold the same dangers only with Kheda and the children. I was now stuck. Even with the war on the verge of ending, we were still going to be outside looking in. I put him off for the moment, thinking I couldn't do anything unless I stayed focused on what I had to do and returned to Kheda alive.

We arrived at Micea right on time. The dignitaries and merchants already landed just as I hoped and were all gathered at the base. The power was working, and all the lights were on. I set the ship down and saw three Kelsairans gather. They meant to arrest me. Sen wanted to go first. I wouldn't let him. They wanted me, and he wouldn't be able to stop them. I could see he was worried for his daughter's sake, but he didn't know just how well she'd taught me.

I opened the hatch and hid on one side. "Come out with your hands up, human. You won't be harmed." He took a step onto the stair. He had a rifle ready to shoot. "You're under arrest. Come out with your hands up." He climbed another step, and his rifle was almost in range.

"This is neutral territory you have no authority here." He turned at the sound of my voice, and I grabbed the barrel of the gun. I pulled him toward me and smashed his nose in with the heel of my hand before knocking him out with the butt of his rifle. I marched down the stairs with the rifle in my hands, and the Kelsairans exchanged a look. "All right, now we all have weapons. I say we do this the old-fashioned way." I offered.

The Kelsairans grinned at one another, thinking I'd lost my mind. They held their guns out to the side as I did the same. The Kelsairans set theirs down gently on the ground, and I let mine drop. They rushed me, and I ducked. I swept the one on the left's legs and punched the right one in the stomach. The one on the ground recovered quickly and got to his feet. He tried to hit me in the jaw, and I blocked. It stung, he was twice as strong as Kheda. I focused on the task at hand just as she taught me falling back on my long hours of meditation. He tried to punch me again, and I sidestepped.

The other Kelsairan was getting up, and I kicked him square in the jaw. He fell to his knees cursing in Kelsairan. The other threw a series of punches at me, and I managed to block or dodged them. He was slow, compared to Kheda. I finally saw an opening and grabbed his wrist. I smashed it with my other elbow, and it broke with little effort. I punched his chest and swept his legs while he was nursing the fractured wrist. He went down and wouldn't be getting up for a while.

I looked at the ship and Sen came out of the hatch. He shook his head realizing who must have taught me to fight. A group of human military police stepped out from behind a ship with guns aimed. They all seemed too shocked to say anything. The man in the center stepped forward. "Well, if you're going to arrest me, then go ahead and try."

He stepped aside. Whether it was out of respect or because he really had no authority or because I beat the crap out of three Kelsairans, I'll never know. But, we walked past them without incidence and into the base.

I knew where they'd be. There was a meeting room large enough to hold them in the south hall. Sen and I made our way there. We were being tracked by cameras I knew, I expected nothing less. The doors opened of their own accord when we were still ten steps from the door. I walked in with Sen a step behind me.

Human, Kelsairan, male and female stared at us as we entered. They were all influential people, either wealthy or in politics. I knew them all by name from their files. "Lieutenant Peterson, we've been expecting you." General Schmidt said plainly. He was the head of human military operations.

"I noticed you're welcome wagon." We were speaking English, but the translators were operating for the Kelsairans. I looked to General Lagis, Schmidt's counterpart for the Kelsairans. "And yours too although I'm afraid your men will need some medical attention. It seems they didn't realize I invited all of you here."

"Senator Ailaryia, we were not expecting you to be here." A little weasel of a Kelsairan spoke up. He was something like their president's aid. His name was Pyia, and he was one of those pulling strings or as close to it as I could safely come on that chain.

"I am here on behalf of my daughter and her husband. Not to mention a cause very dear to me."

"Major Trekes is not allowed to marry." Pyia spat back.

"She wasn't as long as she was in the army, but I think convicting her of treason proved you no longer wanted her," I spoke up. "You threw her into a prison to die, and now you want to claim her as part of your army?"

"What's it to you, human?" General Lagis growled.

"Kheda is my wife," I said clearly. The room was in an uproar, but this wasn't why I came. Sen could see it too.

"We're digressing from the matter at hand what Jackson says is true. He is the soldier she named only as Jeep at her trial. They have been married for nearly a year. Those matters are best left for other times."

I nodded in agreement. "First I want you to know that what you tried on the landing pad was stupid. I'm trying to handle this matter with discretion to avoid civil war on both our planets. Here's the deal. I have dozens of copies of my information stored in numerous places. I have three people waiting to broadcast that information if something happens to me. They need a code from me every five hours. If they don't get it, they broadcast. If you think to harm Kheda or find anyone else in that chain, one of them will broadcast. Got it?"

"What information exactly do you have?" Sharon Davis, the human president's chief of staff asked.

"The best question I've heard all day, Ms. Davis." I moved further into the room and pulled out a chair from the table. "In case you haven't figured it out, I know all of the key players; even the not so obvious ones, like yourself." She looked away unable to keep my gaze. "I know why you fine people meet every so often in remote locations. I know how the war started and, more importantly, why it started." Some of them looked worried others confused.

"We all know why it started." Sean Masden said plainly. He was one of the confused ones. He was an arms dealer, in it merely to make money.

"Apparently not." I looked at General Schmidt who gave me a look like he wanted to eat me alive. "It was simple for the humans. Those in government at the time needed something to rally the people against, and a war would help bolster a failing economy too. Soldiers needed food, clothes, weapons, medical supplies and countless other things."

I looked to General Ligas who was seething equally. "The Kelsairans had similar motives but a little more complicated. You see, they were on the verge of yet another civil war. The governing class that emerged on top of the last war only knew that one way of life. The people, too, were unsatisfied with the peace and quiet on Kelsair. Not to mention there were class issues as well. I don't know all the details; they were fairly good at covering their tracks. I do know enough to put two and two together and follow their logic. They simply fell back on what they knew how to do best."

"The Kelsairan government did no such thing. There were a hundred years of peace and prosperity following the civil war. Only the human's selfish refusal to give up the Sirus System brought it to an end." Senator Merew spoke up. As far as I could tell her only purpose in coming to these meetings was to keep Ligas in check.

"They did; I have proof." I threw a pad on the table with some of the critical documents loaded. She snatched it up and read them. I had them in Kelsairan and English side by side. Her face went blank as she came to realize I wasn't lying.

"Supposing you can prove all this what do you want?" Sharon Davis asked.

"You always ask the best questions. What I want is simple. I want Kheda's, and my name cleared. We both want to be discharged from our respective army and live our lives in peace." She nodded about to speak, but I stopped her. "What we want for everyone else is to end the war."

"You can't simply stop 200 years of fighting." Pyia spat.

"I know, you weasel. But the peace talks have to start now. I already know you can cooperate, or else the body counts would have been higher."

"And why would we want to stop this? Granted I don't like men like you dying but it keeps me rich, and it keeps them in power." Masden spoke up.

"Because if you don't, I'll shut you all down. You'll all be arrested for what you've done."

"No, I don't think so." Pyia spat.

"If they can convict my daughter because she refused to fire on an enemy ship, and supposedly having an affair with a human, then what will the courts think of you conspiring with them to kill your own people?" Sen stared at the man, and he cowered. Sen was right, and the man knew it.

I glared at Ligas "Maybe General Schmidt would be interested in seeing why the Major and I met in the first place."

"And why is that?" Schmidt and Ligas were soldiers through and through forced to play politics by their position. Schmidt was staring at me while still keeping an eye on his adversary.

"I think this is enough for now. I have a code to transmit. You have three hours to talk we'll meet again then to discuss your options." I got up from the table and purposely left the pad. They would read over the few documents it contained and find I had compelling evidence.

I found my way back to the room Kheda slept in while we were here together. Her extra clothes were still neatly folded in the footlocker with a bottle of perfume beside it. I ran my hand over one of her shirts before spraying some of her perfume in the air. I sat on the bed and ran my fingers through my hair missing her terribly. Sen leaned on the door frame. "That's the same scent her mother wore when she was younger. I wouldn't mistake it anywhere. I didn't know Kheda wore perfume though."

"She said she wore it to keep her from feeling too much like a man." I looked up at him suddenly remembering what he'd said in the meeting room. "Kheda and I weren't together until we were married. The tape was a forgery."

"I know. I read her journal, remember? Besides, Ren told me. He seems to like you."

"I think he feels guilty that Bhet nearly killed me during the purification ritual." He laughed, and it wasn't what I expected. I thought of him as a politician and expected a chuckle or half-hearted laugh, but this was a wholehearted belly laugh. Suddenly I felt better.

"Things are going well. They are listening. We will send your message and rest before starting again." He put his arm around me as we headed back to the ship. There was no trouble this time coming or going. It only took a minute to send out the code and was hardly worth the trip. I longed to speak with Kheda, but I knew I couldn't. They would decrypt this message hoping to send out their own in my place, but the code was set to change every time. I was sure to leave that at the end of the message as well, so they knew I knew what they were up to. Kheda was special ops, and I'd been around covert missions long enough to know how they worked.

General Schmidt found me in the hall before I went into the meeting "Maybe when this is over you'd like a job." He'd apparently got my message.

"With all due respect, general, I'm done with the army and the government. So you can shove your job." It didn't get the reaction I wanted, he was still smiling. I hadn't heard the end of it. "Well, what's your decision?" I asked as I came in and sat down again.

"We need more time. We can't make peace in three hours." Pyia was playing stupid.

I played along. "I'm not asking you to. I want you to agree it's possible." They all agreed. "Good, you have 24 hours to announce the location and date of the negotiations to the public."

"But we can't do that. We don't have the authority." Pyia was weaseling again.

"You were asked here for a reason. You're the president's right hand; he can't shit without you. Make it happen Pyia, or I expose all of you." They all stared at Pyia.

"We want all of your copies of these documents Lieutenant." Ms. Davis demanded.

"You will as soon as I have a signed peace treaty. For now, I can give you one full copy a piece."

"There's more?" She countered.

"Much more to that matter plus a file on each of you for good measure." She shook her head in disbelief. "Generals, I trust you've both been thinking of good stories to clear my wife's and my name."

"It won't be easy," Ligas replied. He was right about that. The Kelsairans made a mess out of the whole situation.

"No, but our discharges should be."

"Already done. Are you in a hurry to get somewhere?" Schmidt asked.

"I have a wife waiting for me. I'm leaving first thing in the morning. You've heard my demands you've seen my evidence what happens from here is up to you."

"And if you and Trekes mysteriously die?"

"Then one of my other copies is broadcast. Never fear, general; there will be work for you for many years to come. Peace does not come easily after 200 years of spreading hatred and lies. There will be some resistance on both sides, and the government will need your help enforcing the new found peace. At least now you'll know you're fighting for something worthwhile."

I left them with something to think about. Change took time, and it was going to be hard, but it was worth it in the long run. I hoped my children would never feel the loss of a sibling by the hate of a person they'd never met.

Chapter 22

I walked the perimeter of the island that night entirely alone thinking of the time Kheda and I spent here. This is the place the war ended for us. It was only fitting that this is where it ended for everyone else. This was the place I realized everything the government told me was a lie. I remember looking at Kheda and seeing a woman and not a Kelsairan. She was someone to be loved, not hated. The war was over for me then, even if it was just with her. Over the next few months, my men could tell something was wrong. My heart wasn't in it anymore. I think that was the reason we were caught on that ridge. I knew then it was my fault and that's why I stayed behind. That's why I was captured, and that's how Kheda came back into my life.

The next morning, I brought one copy to Pyia and Ms. Davis. Pyia took his and slinked away. Ms. Davis lingered keeping me trapped there. "The announcement is set for 13:00 hours today. The talks will be held here in three weeks. I hope you can join us."

"I have a previous engagement," I said simply not wanting to reveal that the babies should be coming around that time. I was afraid if anyone knew they'd come after us and we'd be on the run again. Ms. Davis looked at the pad in her hands.

"How did you get this?"

I sighed. "Months of my life trapped in a room behind computers."

"Was it worth it?" What she really wanted to know is if Kheda was worth it.

"She means more to me than anything in the world."

"I spoke with the president, and he apologizes for your treatment during this situation. He wants to..."

"Save it, I don't need long-winded apologies. I need to get back to my family."

"Are you sure you don't have a little time to spare?" She was making a pass at me.

"I'm sure." I walked away from her not wanting to stay a moment longer. I'd nearly made it on to my ship when I heard General Schmidt behind me.

"Aren't you forgetting these?" he held out two pieces of paper. Our discharge orders. "General Ligas wanted to come as well, but it seems he didn't want to lose Trekes especially not to a human."

"Thanks," I took the orders and headed inside.

"You're going to be news in an hour. Oh, and Jackson, I want you to know I'll have my best man tracking you down about the job." I nodded. His best man was Jeannie. She'd find me every so often, offer me the job and I'll refuse. In the meantime, I'd have an excuse to see her. Although, he didn't know I knew Jeannie was MI. Even if he knew of our involvement, her job was classified. This would be a fun game of cat and mouse.

Sen was already at the controls waiting to take off. I sat down beside him and closed the hatch. "Do you want to see Kheda's handiwork in action?" he nodded. Once we were out of Micea's atmosphere we pushed the engines to the limit, he was impressed. This ship wasn't meant to go this fast, and he knew it. We raced back to Aran but it was still a three-week trip, I could only hope I made it in time to see my children born. We watched the monitors as news came up about Kheda or me or any signs of the peace to come. It was just as Schmidt and Davis said.

The Kelsairans claimed I escaped Kras with a different Kelsairan woman, a big-time player never meant to get out. They said I killed her in self-defense when she tried to kill me. I'd supposedly been on the run since not knowing where to turn because of my supposed involvement with Trekes. She, on the other hand, had been sitting in

Roteo exactly where they said she was supposed to go and this had all been a paperwork nightmare and case of mistaken identity. Trekes was released from prison for good behavior and been honorably discharged. The army gave me credit for time served in Kras and on the run, and my term of service was shortened by a year. I too was given an honorable discharge.

If I hadn't been at the center of it all, I wouldn't have believed it. I could only wonder what the public thought. It didn't really matter. My name was officially clear, and so was Kheda's. Her record would only say failure to obey orders and when it came to refusing to fire on innocents that were nothing to be ashamed of. Besides, our children and families knew the truth, and that was most important.

We set down on Aran a little under three weeks after leaving Micea. Aya was waiting at the secondary landing pad with a land cruiser. The first thing he asked about was his ship. I grinned at him and asked about Kheda. Sen climbed in behind us, and Aya sped off up the hill. Aya wouldn't say much about Kheda, and he had me a little worried. I barely got my boots off before rushing inside.

Ren greeted me at the door. "Where are you off to in such a hurry Jackson?"

"Kheda is she all right?"

"She is resting and so are the babies." He looked to Aya. "For shame Aya, letting him worry." Ren took me by the arm "Go wash up then you may see them."

"They're here? Both of them?" I couldn't breathe for a moment.

"Alive and well, but you must wash the sand off first." He was right. I was covered once again with sand from the dreadful winds. Bhet came to show me where to wash up. I don't think I'd ever showered so quickly in my life. Not only was Kheda waiting for me, but so were my children. I longed to have all three of them in my arms.

Kheda was in a small room on the lower level where it was cooler. She sat up in bed with a baby in her arms and another asleep beside her.

She looked up when I came in, and I knew she wanted to get up to greet me, but she also didn't want to wake the children. "God, Jackson; I'm so glad to see you."

I rushed to her side and hugged her as best I could with the baby in her arms. I kissed her savoring the feel of her lips on mine once more. I let her go and looked at the sleeping child in her arms amazed. "Your daughter, Saleena Dynia." She laid the tiny child in my arms and readjusted her before picking up the other infant. "Your son, Sen Michael." She placed him on my other arm, and my heart swelled. She wrapped her arms around me from behind and lay her head on my shoulder. "They'll be a week old tomorrow."

"I see you couldn't wait for me."

"If I could have waited, then I would have, so I could have yelled at you in person." Saleena opened her eyes at the sound of my voice. She stared up at me with opaque blue eyes, her mother's eyes. She settled into my arm and fell asleep again. Her hair was thick and black, much the same as mine was when I was born. Sen's, though, was light and more like peach fuzz.

"She knows you. She cries when Aya holds her and even Ren sometimes."

"It's because I talked to them every night. Where does the blonde hair come from?" I smiled down at my daughter.

She ran her hand through Sen's hair, and he looked at both of us. His eyes were the same blue as his mother and sister. "My mother swears it's from her."

I swallowed the lump in my throat. "Your mother is here?" Kheda nodded. "She doesn't like me very much."

"She is adjusting; she has grandchildren because of you." Someone knocked on the door. "I swear she can hear through walls. You mention her, and she appears."

"Speak of the devil," I commented, and Kheda smacked my shoulder. "Come in," I called.

Kheda's mother wasn't very tall for a Kelsairan at 5'10," but she was all legs just like her daughter. She had a mane of long blonde hair held back with a clip at the base of her neck. She wore a plain lavender dress, but her presence demanded attention. Her eyes were a piercing grey with a few spots of blue. I moved to get up, but she stopped me. "No need to get up. I see you have your hands full. I only came to introduce myself. It's only fitting since you married my daughter."

Her tone was cold, but I could tell she was making a real effort for her grandchildren's sake, if not mine. "My entire family speaks very highly of you, Jackson. It's obvious you care a great deal for my daughter. I would like to get to know you so I may overcome my prejudices. Would you allow me to do so?"

I looked to Kheda, stunned. "Of course I would." She smiled at me, amused. "You didn't believe I could speak Kelsairan, did you?"

"They told me you could but," she shrugged. "I'm sorry; this will be hard for me. Will you forgive a stubborn woman in advance?"

"If you promise me one thing." She stared at me "Never say anything to discredit me or undermine me in front of my children."

She nodded. "Of course not, Kheda; you chose wisely." She left us alone, and Kheda stared at me.

"That took a lot for her to come here like that."

"I know it did. Trust me, I appreciate the effort, but I won't have her undermining me with the children."

"You sized her up rather well, she already favors Sen."

"Just as she favored Aya. She loves you Kheda, but she pushed you into your life for his sake."

"I know, and I let her, but it worked out for the best. We just won't let her do it with our children." She took Saleena from me and laid her in a pile of blankets. "Take a nap with me before they get hungry." She took Sen as well and laid him next to his sister.

Late that night I couldn't sleep. I got out of bed without disturbing Kheda or the babies. I sat in a chair staring at all three of them. I must have sat there an hour before finally digging out a pad and writing in my journal.

As I sit here now, on a foreign world with my wife and children, I can't help but wonder what the future holds for any of us. I have no job or home to speak of. My wife is a different race, and my children are half of her and half of me. That makes us outsiders no matter where we go. Even with the peace negotiations, there is still 200 years of animosity to overcome. Yet, somehow I can't help being optimistic. Kheda and I did the impossible, and if we could stop a war, we could raise a family as unique as ours.

So that brings me to the end of my story, and the beginning of a new one. I sit at the end of an undistinguished career in the United Human Army and find my proudest moment was saving a Kelsairan woman from a burning ship. Our two peoples sit at a pivotal time in our history, and I can only hope we all do what's best for the next generation. While mine and Kheda's version of events will most likely remain hidden for years to come our story is still worth hearing. I'm writing this now so future generations can see what happens when we learn to look past the hate and work together. I'm writing this so that my children can hold their heads high when they think of their parents. We were a Kelsairan and a human who chose to love one another and find a better way of life. We were soldiers who chose peace.

A Note From the Author

As an author, I work hard to craft entertaining and well written books for my readers. If you can spare just a moment of your time, please leave a short review of my book. I would greatly appreciate it.

Let everyone know how much you enjoyed Neutral Space.

Please feel free to contact me directly through any of my social media.

Social Media Contacts

Website: https://rtranbooks.net/

https://asmallgangofauthors.blogspot.com/

Facebook page: https://m.facebook.com/Rtranbooks/

Twitter: https://twitter.com/rtranbooks/

email: rtranbooks.com@outlook.com

Goodreads: https://www.goodreads.com/author/show/16335980.R_Tran

Also by Rebecca Tran

Box Set
Dragons of the North

Chronicles of the Coranydas
A Guardian Falls
The Rashade'

Dragons of the South
Hunted
Sweet Surrender
Primal Instincts

Standalone
Neutral Space
Magic Always Has a Price
Honor Bound
For Their Sins

Watch for more at rtranbook.net.

About the Author

Rebecca Tran is an award-winning author, reviewer and blogger. She started writing when she was sixteen as self-prescribed therapy after her father passed away and hasn't stopped since. Rebecca is also a pharmacist, and mother to two rambunctious girls and a Boston Terrier and Pitt Bull. If she ever has free time she likes combing resale shops to add to her teapot collection or quilting. Currently, she lives in her home state of Missouri.

Read more at rtranbook.net.